Shadow Tag

Also by Louise Erdrich

Novels

Love Medicine
The Beet Queen
Tracks
The Crown of Columbus (with Michael Dorris)
The Bingo Palace
Tales of Burning Love
The Antelope Wife
The Last Report on the Miracles at Little No Horse
The Master Butchers Singing Club
Four Souls
The Painted Drum
The Plague of Doves

Stories

The Red Convertible: New and Selected Stories, 1978–2008

Poetry

Jacklight
Baptism of Desire
Original Fire

For Children

Grandmother's Pigeon
The Birchbark House
The Range Eternal
The Game of Silence
The Porcupine Year

Nonfiction

The Blue Jay's Dance
Books and Islands in Ojibwe Country

Shadow Tag

LOUISE ERDRICH

HARPER

An Imprint of **HarperCollins** *Publishers*

This is a work of fiction. The characters, incidents, and dialogues are products of the author's imagination and are not to be construed as real. Any resemblance to actual persons, living or dead, is entirely coincidental.

Designed by Kathryn Parise

ISBN 978-1-61664-745-2

Shadow Tag

Part I

November 2, 2007

BLUE NOTEBOOK

I have two diaries now. The first is the hardbound red Daily Reminder of the type I have been writing in since 1994, when we had Florian. You gave me the first book in order to record my beginning year as a mother. It was very sweet of you. I have written in a book like it ever since. They are hidden in the bottom of a drawer in my office, covered with ribbons and wrapping paper. The latest, the one that interests you at present, is kept in the very back of a file cabinet containing old bank statements, checks left over from defunct accounts, the sorts of things we both vow to shred every year but end up stuffing into files. After quite a lot of searching, I expect, you have found my red diary. You have been reading it in order to discover whether I am deceiving you.

The second diary, what you might call my real diary, is the one I am writing in now.

Today I left the house and drove to the branch of the Wells Fargo Bank that is located in uptown Minneapolis beneath the Sons of Norway Hall. I parked in the customer lot and walked in, through two sets of glass doors, down a spiral staircase, to the safe-deposit desk. I tapped a little bell and a woman named Janice appeared. She assisted me in the purchase of a medium-size security box. I paid cash for a year's rental and signed my name, three times for signature verification, on the deposit-box card. I took the key Janice offered. She matched my key to another key and let me into the safe-deposit area. After we slid my box from its place in the wall, she ushered me into one of three private little closets, each containing no more than a desk-height shelf and chair. I closed the door to my private room and removed this blue notebook from the big black leather bag that you gave me for Christmas. Ten or fifteen minutes passed before I could begin. My heart was beating so fast. I couldn't tell if I was experiencing panic, grief, or, possibly, happiness.

As soon as the sound of Irene's car motor vanished into the general low din of the city, Gil sat up. The towel he used to shade his eyes slipped off his face. He often lay down on his studio couch when he needed to refresh his eyes, and sometimes dozed off. He could sleep there for as long as an hour, but more often he jerked awake after fifteen minutes, refreshed and startled, as though he'd been dipped in a cool underground stream. He sat up patting for his eyeglasses, which he sometimes balanced on his chest. Sure enough, the wire ovals had fallen onto the floor. He retrieved them, hooked them behind his ears. His thick hair started low on his brow and he swept it straight back, smoothed and retied his short, gray ponytail. He stepped up to the painting of his wife and regarded it. His eyes were close-set, cold, curious, and dark. He pressed a knuckle to his chin. His thin cheeks were flecked with yellow paint.

He peered at Irene's likeness, then he frowned and looked away, blinking like a person who can't quite make out some figure in the distance. Suddenly he bent over, and added a few tense strokes. He stood back, wrapped his brush in an oiled cloth, then put the brush and palette into a Ziploc bag. He deposited the bag in a small refrigerator. Descending hungrily, he left his studio and went downstairs to the kitchen. He took the one can of Coke he allowed himself per day from the refrigerator. Sipping, he descended the rest of the way and entered his wife's basement office. He went at once to the sand-colored metal file cabinet and opened a drawer labeled Old Accts.

November 1, 2007

RED DIARY

W hat an odd day this is with the house so empty and Gil upstairs endlessly reworking a painting. I expect he is having trouble asking me to sit for him again. Flo and Stoney are okay now after fever. Riel never gets sick, but she is having a difficult time at school this year. Stoney is making a board game for some afterschool project that involves the habits of black bears. Very Minnesota. I think I'm going to lose my mind over what I'm doing.

He actually thought he could feel the blood drain from his heart when he read those words. *I think I'm going to lose my mind over what I'm doing.* He put his head down on the cool oak of Irene's desk, but then thought, as he always did when he came across some hidden reference to the other man, what the hell did I expect? I let myself in for this. I looked for this. He tried to discipline his reaction, and forced himself to consider other explanations: she could be referring to her history thesis. Or that old article on Louis Riel. Before the children, she had published several pieces that were considered brilliant; she was a very promising scholar. Her work had included new material that shed light on Riel's mental states. She'd kept working after Florian was born. But after she became pregnant again, she had abandoned her work—except that she'd named their daughter after the depressed Metis patriot, a man to whom his own family was distantly related. Riel was eleven. And now that Stoney was in first grade, Irene was trying to finish her Ph.D. thesis, so that she could start looking for a job. Her subject was now the nineteenth-century painter of Native Americana George Catlin.

Perhaps she was suffering from academic frustration? Losing her mind—over George Catlin's clumsy, repetitive, earnest depictions of people—all of whom would sicken and die soon after. Gil himself could not bear to look at Catlin's work. The tragic irony of it offended him. And for Irene, a poor excuse.

I think I'm going to lose my mind. Well, good, it proved that something remained of Irene's conscience. She deserved to suffer somehow—secretly, internally, if not publicly—for what she was doing to them all. Careless, careless, reckless!

He reared up, slammed his hands down. A few drops were flung from the can of soda, but it did not tip over. He drank it all before he put the diary back exactly the way he'd found it. He thought of dialing Irene's cell phone, but he doubted she would answer it. Irene grew restless in the afternoons and did errands before she picked up the children. She always returned with some loud proof of what she had accomplished—a bag of groceries, a plastic tub, deposit slips. Or she exercised— she was strong and had an offhand self-confidence about her body. She thought she could do anything. She was an excellent swimmer. There was, of course, nothing wrong with that. Plenty of athletic people were emotional wrecks. He shook his head and squeezed his eyes shut.

Irene America was over a decade his junior and had been the subject of his paintings in all of her incarnations—thin and virginal, a girl, then womanly, pregnant, naked, de- murely posed or frankly pornographic. He'd named each por- trait after her. *America 1. America 2. America 3. America 4* had just sold in six figures. If only he'd kept some of the earliest, the best portraits. They were selling for more. The series was becoming famous, or was already famous. Before Irene, he'd painted landscapes, reservation scenes that reminded people of Hopper. He'd been called a Native Edward Hopper—irritat- ing. He hadn't gone to art school, but he'd read, and painted, and painted, and observed. And then he lived in New York for two years, working for galleries, installations for other art- ists. Every night he'd gone home and spent his evenings at his own work. For a time he'd taught at a small college. But the students had seemed conceited and entitled. He lost patience with them. He'd scrounged together a little money and started painting full-time. The paintings sold. He did not look back. He'd become successful, if not widely known. He was an artist who could support a family with his work—no small feat. But now he was losing confidence and control. His paintings were hiding from him because Irene was hiding something. He could see it in the opacity of her eyes, the insolence of her flesh, the impatient weariness of her body when she let down her guard. She'd ceased to love him. Her gaze was an airless void.

Gil was still sitting at Irene's desk when the children slammed through the door upstairs, throwing off their coats, stepping out of their boots. He heard their backpacks thud just over his head and then their footsteps fading toward the kitchen. They were quieter, opening the refrigerator, murmuring as they grazed. Irene kept the snack drawer and fridge stuffed with food that could be eaten immediately, while Gil bought dried beans, rice, frozen meat, pasta in huge quantities, and kept his stashes deep in the cupboards and freezer. Now he heard the children rummaging around like squirrels, their paws in the cellophane bags of cookies and chips. He thought of going upstairs and stopping them, but before he made a move they'd pounded up the stairway to their rooms and things were quiet again.

For years now, he thought, he had been mourning a death without knowing exactly who had died or how it had come about. He had felt the grief in their lovemaking first, but got used to it. She gave him pleasure, but they'd stopped searching each other's faces and the words of arousal they both used seemed perfunctory. Then, over time, making love became something darker, more painful.

It was as if she weren't really there, but watching him from underwater. He had the notion that she'd gone to wrestle with some deep interior drama whose plot he would learn only after it was resolved. He already feared the outcome would not be in his favor. So he tried. But he could get her attention only by force, in bed, and he found their anger—scratching, biting, even striking each other—both torrid and embarrassing. On days he didn't have the strength to woo her with surprise gifts, he used the children to get to her. He'd blow some little crisis out of proportion. But afterward she always slipped through his fingers again.

Once upon a time she had been eager to sit for him. There had been a softly electric quality, a constantly changing force field, between them while he painted. Gil had given his entire attention to her youth first, but after that he devotedly painted the effect of experience on flesh. The imprint of his own mouth on Irene's mouth. Age, time. Snow slipping off a tree limb until it crashed whitely down. Irene's weary softness after giving birth. Her breasts, hot with fever as her milk came in, swollen to a gorgeous size and so sensitive that her milk let down at the lightest touch. She'd nursed in his studio, naked, with pillows to prop the baby, and he'd have two paintings going, one for each side as she changed. That was happiness. After the babies became toddlers, then small children, he painted her body as it drew back into itself and toughened. For a time, he'd abandoned her and painted other subjects. But he'd been working on a mythic level with the portraits—her portrayals immediately evoked problems of exploitation, the indigenous body, the devouring momentum of history. More than that—he'd progressed to a technical level that allowed him an almost limitless authority. Abstract expressionism had been the tyranny of the day, but he'd stuck defiantly with figurative painting and now his control of old master techniques looked almost radical.

Irene's distance aroused in Gil a desolate craving. Her secrets drove him to a manic despondency in which he began to do the best work of his life. No matter what her sin, he believed he saw her with pure eyes. People called him a charming hypocrite, but in his art he wanted only to get at the truth. So how could he blame her body, he thought, painting himself into the picture, himself in the mirror like Velázquez, like Degas creeping up on a prostitute in her bath. If his brush were merely the eyelash of a cat and he had one canvas to work on for the rest of his life, it would be a painting of Irene.

She had loved him intensely. She had looked up to him and trusted him. She had believed that he was the most extraordinary man in the world. Actually, she still said this. Only she said it now in a way he found patronizing.

He stood and pushed the chair back. He stretched, picked up the can, and closed the door carefully as he made his way back up the stairs. It was his night to cook. The man she was seeing didn't cook. He was pretty sure of that. He didn't even know how she could really be seeing the man he suspected, a man who'd been Gil's friend. Germaine lived about a thousand six hundred and fifty-two miles away, on a hillside in Seattle with his wife, Lissa, a vulnerable humanitarian whose good works fortunately took her around the world without him. Germaine Okestaf-Becker had a joint name, yoked by a hyphen, which was all so barfingly PC. Plus he was more Indian than Gil, three-quarters as opposed to one-quarter, and so Germaine had him by a half quantum, which was a big plus as mixed-blood women are generally suckers for darker men and Irene probably was too, though she was careful not to say so. Yet Gil was pretty sure he was more than sexually adequate—in crude terms, well never mind . . . she'd chosen after all to have her children with him. Native women of whatever blood quantum are extremely discriminating about the men they have their children with, not only because of genes and so forth but because of tribal enrollment issues and government treaty-right benefits, which extend even to eventual college preference. Having children was the big thing.

Irene must have loved him very much to have his children when his tribal roots—a mishmash of Klamath and Cree and landless Montana Chippewa—weren't recognized. So of course he had no casino per cap and had to live by his art. He was pretty sure she had married him for his art and then slowly found that his art was no fun to live with. His talent was not him; his talent made him boring, as a person, and he drank too much at night because the concentrations of his day exhausted him. But then, increasingly, so did she—drink too much *and* exhaust him.

He was drained now, and lonely for Irene. This intercalary hour between her day and his day made him feel invisible. He poured himself a glass of wine and looked around the kitchen, focused. He took eggs, butter, aged cheddar, milk from the refrigerator. A few weeks ago, Irene had said something about a cheese soufflé. He'd surprise her; she'd love it. He took out his favorite cookbook, held the page open with a transparent weighted page marker especially for cooks, and began to follow the directions with extreme care. He loved cooking, like laundry, because something done perfectly according to instructions could have immediate and positive results.

Gil surveyed the organized table. Very satisfying. Green plates, yellow napkins. The cheese soufflé. Crusty baguette. A fresh salad of baby spinach, toasted walnuts, pears. A bottle of chilled white.

So, what did everyone do today? asked Gil. Stoney, you first.

Stoney was a shy six-year-old with a bewildered way of shaking the shaggy hair that curled behind his ears. His eyes were lighter than his skin, which would one day make him strikingly attractive. Right now, he was confused, awkward, and one of his bottom front right teeth was missing. Gil saw his son as another artist already. He saw himself in Stoney's natural love of drawing and painting. At the same time, he envied his son's advantages and even coveted the handsome materials that Irene bought for him. Sometimes Gil picked up a thick piece of paper that Stoney had discarded after only a few pencil marks. Gil brought these cast-offs up to his own studio to use and re-membered drawing with a ratty ballpoint pen, the stub of a pencil, or a wax marker stolen from the grocery store. His own first works were scratched out on scraps of cardboard, the inside of macaroni and cereal boxes, and on wrapping paper rescued from a store's trash.

What did you say? What did you do? Gil asked Stoney.

I painted.

What did you paint?

Like, scenes. For a play.

We don't begin sentences with *like*. Could you rephrase that?

Stoney's glance flickered from side to side for help. Irene put her hand on Gil's arm, patted his wrist until he looked at her.

Scenes for a play.

Complete sentence?

Stoney painted a scene for a play, Gil. That's a cool thing for a six-year-old to do. Irene took some salad, and then said in a more ingratiating tone, Your soufflé is amaz-ing. You're a great cook!

Who would think an artist of such stature could also deal so brilliantly with the humble egg? said Florian. His face was faunlike, subtle with malice. Of them all, he looked most like Gil.

Gil turned back to Stoney. How is your black bear project coming?

It's not black bears, Daddy.

Oh? It's not? What is it?

Wolves.

Irene's fork paused over a crescent of Bosc pear. She put her fork down beside her plate. Wolves. Black bears. She'd made the same mistake in her diary, and written it down. She sat there staring at her plate for so long that Gil looked at her. She was breathing quickly.

Are you all right?

I don't feel well, said Irene.

The children's faces froze; they looked extremely frightened. Riel—raffish, sloppy Riel—started up from her chair to touch her mother's sleeve.

Mommy . . .

I'm all right, really, just a little headache! Sudden! I have to go. . . .

Their heads craned after her as she left the room.

Don't gawk, said Gil. He poured the rest of the wine into his glass. And don't finish your milk until after you finish your meal. Florian, your salad?

Yes, Dad.

Just one piece of bread, Riel, and go easy on the butter.

Is Mom okay?

In many ways, yes, in some ways, no. Now stop asking questions.

November 2, 2007

BLUE NOTEBOOK

Y ou'd grown careless and I'd been having these odd feelings for a while. As though you were reading my mind or anticipating my thoughts. You were meticulous about replacing my diary exactly as you'd found it and also disturbing nothing in my room. But it was more than that. I couldn't imagine it. It was a failure of imagination on my part. Or at least I thought so at first. But now, as I sit here in this little bank closet, I realize that I didn't include many truths in my red diary. And I hid it. I must have known you would not be able to resist looking inside, trying to find the secret.

You have painted me for nearly fifteen years. In that time, I have had secrets. I have let them rest like dragonflies on the surface of my body. Once, you even painted an elaborate, transparent, veined wing on my inner thigh and I thought—he sees!

Our children were born into your hands. What more can there be for you to know?

I have been taught to think that life proceeds inevitably from its formative starting point and that its course is difficult to change. If it's the same with love, then there were bad omens from the beginning: The night before our wedding I dreamed that I was savagely attacked and pulled apart by wild dogs. You hardly knew your father and your mother had a strange weakness all through the left side of her body that made her tilt toward you in a sinister way. You are an unlucky thirteen years older than me. But here is the most telling thing: you wish to possess me. And my mistake: I loved you and let you think you could.

After I left the pleasant dinner you had prepared, I walked downstairs to my office and drew up the chair. Black bears. Wolves. And the soufflé. It was transparent. I put my hand on the cool oak of my desk and touched the circle where you'd set your can and noticed the tacky place where you hadn't wiped up the sugary spill.

Irene went upstairs to the kitchen and did the dishes that the children had carefully stacked on the counter. They were in their rooms doing homework now. She would bring them down one by one and go over their lessons and piano lessons. Gil was watching CNN just off the kitchen, in the den. The sound was off and he was talking on the telephone. Things were proceeding inexorably toward bedtime. The dogs were sleeping in the hallway, in front of the main staircase.

Wherever the family was, these two dogs, both six-year-old shepherd mixes, took up their posts at the central coming-and-going point. Gil called them concierge dogs. And it's true, they were inquisitive and accommodating. But they were not fawning or overly playful. They were watchful and thoughtful. Irene thought they had gravitas. Weighty demeanors. She thought of them as diplomats. She had noticed that when Gil was about to lose his temper one of the dogs always appeared and did something to divert his attention. Sometimes they acted like fools, but it was brilliant acting. Once, when he was furious about a bill for the late fees for a lost video, one of the dogs had walked right up to Gil and lifted his leg over his shoe. Gil was shouting at Florian when the piss splattered down, and she'd felt a sudden jolt of pride in the dog.

Once the children were asleep, Irene slipped into the bathroom, locked the door, ran a bath, and lowered herself into the stinging water. It was a long, deep, old-fashioned tub and Irene could lift her hips slightly and stretch her legs to the lapping overflow drain. If she had been born an Indian two hundred years ago, she hoped she'd have been lucky enough to belong to a tribe with a hot spring. She would have fought the whiteman fiercely for a hot soak. A life without hot water would be hard to bear. She supposed this made her a weak creature, greedy for comfort, in some ways limited. But it was not just the blissful sting of the water. It was her nakedness. That she could be alone with her nakedness. And there was no demand on her nakedness, not from her husband, whose reaction to her nakedness was much too complex, nor from her babies, who when they were toddlers thought her nakedness a happy joke, or even from the mirror, which demanded that she assess her nakedness as a woman does, through the eyes of others.

When she went out with Gil, she cultivated an air of neglect. She knew she was an arresting woman, even so. She wore her hair coarsely tangled and painstakingly applied unfashionable shades of makeup. Bright green eye shadow. Heliotrope lipstick. Rouge. Sometimes she powdered her face thickly white, like a geisha. She was rangy, dark, tall, and inarticulate. An art dealer had called her pantherlike and Gil had repeated this for weeks, amused, but Irene had liked to think of herself as alluring in her silence, rather than awkward and tongue-tied. Any power she owned lay in her feigned indifference.

She had to shed the weight of Gil's eyes. Exist unobserved. That way she could gradually soothe the ache of self awareness. The baths were therefore spiritual. They didn't simply cleanse, they restored. Irene could sink her awareness into purely physical sensations—weightless ease, the languid suspension of her hands, the light sweat at her forehead, her scalp tight as a cap, the slight burning behind her closed eyelids, the panic beating in her throat.

The words were still in his mind, *I think I'm going to lose my mind over what I'm doing*, when Gil tapped on the bathroom door.

Can I come in?

It's locked. I'm in the bathtub.

What are you doing?

Taking a bath.

For how long?

I'm reading, too.

What are you reading?

Irene swirled the water over her breasts, and frowned at the door.

A diary, she finally called.

Gil was silent, but she knew he was still there.

Oh? Whose?

Irene thought for a moment.

The diary of Christopher Columbus, the one he kept on his first voyage?

Oh really? Gil leaned against the door jamb. They could hear each other perfectly.

He mentions his first encounter with a human being from the New World—a young girl who swims out to his ship. You remember? An emblematic moment, Gil, are you still there?

Yes.

Have you ever wondered what happened to the girl? Did he make her a slave, or did she succumb to an Old World disease? None of her tribe survived ten years. How was she killed? Women are always swimming trustingly out to men! We're curious as otters when we should be wary as snakes.

Irene gave a strange, light laugh that echoed hollowly against the tiles. Gil turned away from the door, in a fury.

How can you say that! He walked away, too softly for her to hear. You are the snake! You have struck poison into my heart!

As soon as he thought *snake, poison*, Gil was taken with an idea. He walked upstairs to his studio and stood in front of a wooden panel that he was going to use. Gil always kept a number of paintings going at once. He loved to paint on wood, although it was hard to get good pieces and he preferred not to use Masonite. He haunted lumberyards and salvage yards and reuse stores. Sometimes an old door of solid oak made its way into his hands from a St. Paul mansion. White oak. The Mona Lisa had been painted on white poplar. He loved to paint on doors. He might saw them in half, sand them down, change their shape. But when he painted on a piece of wood that had once been a door, something of the original function of the door came into the painting. It opened and closed, as the door had. The aura of its doorness, mysterious possibilities, the act of stepping into a new room—all of that remained faintly in the picture.

Gil had already prepared his panel, painted it with rabbit glue, then gesso, then sanded it, then repeated the process layer after layer until he had a silken surface. Now he stood in front of the blank panel. He sat for an hour, staring at it. He went away and came back, made a few marks, left, returned. He was seeing and rejecting compositions. He had to pass through hundreds, thousands sometimes, before he actually set his scene up or posed Irene or went out and made more drawings, brought them back, tried them out. Collected his picture until it became definite and filled his mind. The snake, the poison, the hatred. He was thinking those things. Gil's hatred was a useful fuel, it cinched his focus and brought clarity. Where was the truth? The panel was an open question. He stepped close and sketched a few light shapes. His heart was beating quickly. He sat down again. He turned his head. His ferrety, clever, attractive features were intently fixed.

Suddenly, Gil smelled his mother walking into the house from work at the church basement. She was not really there of course, but the smell she always had when she returned from work hit him. In that basement church secondhand store, she sorted through donations to the Indian mission— old vinyl records and sweat-stained bras, broken shoes and castaway dishes. She had always smelled of used things, a must of poverty. But it was strongest when she came in from work. In her arms she carried magazines for him, books, and anything to do with art. She stole blank paper from the priest's office, pencils. He made his own charcoal drawing sticks by burning twigs. He drew incessantly, secretly. His fingers moved at all times as he copied what he saw onto the skin of his arm, the fabric of his trousers, the pitted varnish on the top of his desk.

His mother had loved the drawings and saved them in a box that she kept underneath her bed. When he was Riel's age, a chill had entered one side of her body. It became a palsy. Her mouth drooped, her eye; soon it affected her hip and shoulder. She just kept on getting more and more lopsided until one day she'd toppled over. He'd stood her up like a huge doll and from then on she'd walked with a tottering marionette gait, still tipping from time to time.

They'd lived in Havre. They lived in Bismarck and Rapid City. They lived in Billings and they'd lived nowhere, just a place once, in the country, in an old house where they'd been stranded without a car and eaten all of the dandelion greens in the yard. On the farm, they had netted pigeons with an old nylon curtain, clubbed them dead, and roasted them. They'd found an accordion, blankets, pots, a stained mattress, and a paint set in that house. The first time Gil squeezed the paint from a tube, yellow paint, it had seemed to him luscious and his mouth had watered.

His breath came quickly and his mouth was dry now as he sketched the lurching woman, the fallen woman, the woman he was picking up and setting on her feet, and the woman falling again. All of this was in the one figure of Irene. The knowing of what he wanted, the strain of seeing it in his mind, the excitement of making it visible cramped his fingers. He put the pencil down and wrung out his hand to relax his grip.

She was asleep by the time he crawled into bed. They under-stood that their bodies were not accessible if either of them waited until the lights were out. They had never discussed this, but over time they had trained each other in a thousand ways. They had been training each other since 1992, the year of their impromptu wedding. Gil settled himself against the curved wall of her back, turned away from him in sleep. Habit soothed him. No matter what the day had brought, Irene's sleeping presence gave him comfort. The dark, mammal weight of her in the bed made him drowsy. Her unconscious-ness was sweet to him, and he let himself drift on the tide of her breathing.

The morning was routine. The dogs waited patiently until the family came downstairs, and then they were let out into the yard. Gil made coffee in a French press. He added a teaspoon of sugar and a little milk to his and gave Irene her coffee black. She walked upstairs with hers while downstairs Gil put out the cereal in bowls and arranged the spoons and glasses of orange juice. Once everyone was in the kitchen, he buttered whole wheat toast and set the toast directly on the children's plates while it was still warm and crisp. Florian and Riel ate quickly. Stoney tried to keep up with them. Irene foraged out the things they needed in their backpacks—sneakers for gym day, snow pants, library books. She gathered their coats, mittens, and boots by the door and threw on her monster coat, a white thing made of quilted down that looked like a sleeping bag with arms. Yetilike, she walked the dogs and the children out to the corner and waited until the bus picked them up. She observed a small superstition: she stood motionless until the bus had passed out of her sight. She did this out of an unexamined belief that her vigilance would keep them safe all day. She then continued walking the dogs. Her pockets were always stuffed with Liver Snaps and plastic bags. Today she walked them all the way to the lake and back. She took a long walk to avoid sharing coffee and the morning paper and planning the day out with Gil. She needed to make her own plans. She had decided not to confront him about reading her diary. In the past, she would have done so. But on her walk something occurred to her. Her thoughts veered off, then went toward it again and again.

If Gil didn't know that she knew about him reading her diary, she could write things there to manipulate him. Even hurt him. She thought she would start with a simple test, some irresistible hook.

That night they all watched a movie. Even Florian watched it, slouching in a chair behind the rest of his family. *The Parent Trap* is about two female twins, each unaware of the other's existence, each sent to live apart from the other with an estranged parent. The twins meet by chance at a summer camp, change places, and plot to make their parents fall in love and eventually remarry. Irene found the movie painful to watch because the parents get back together in the end. Gil found the movie poignant because the twins were played by Lindsay Lohan, so clever and bright back then. He loved the end and squeezed Irene's hand. After the movie, although it was late, Irene went downstairs. She had decided what to write in her diary, for Gil to see.

November 2, 2007

RED DIARY

Tonight we watched a movie and Gil made his special butter-and-herb popcorn. The parents in the movie had not broken up for serious reasons and had little trouble falling back in love. It must be very difficult for Gil to understand why I cannot simply backspace emotionally and fall back in love, the way those parents did. Why can't I recover the feelings I had at the beginning? Infatuation, sudden attraction, is partly a fever of surfaces, an absence of knowledge. Falling in love is also falling into knowledge. Enduring love comes when we love most of what we learn about the other person and can tolerate the faults they cannot change. I stopped loving Gil abruptly before Stoney was born. On that day, he did something intolerable. I wonder if he remembers what he did? He probably can't imagine that something so ordinary, something he does every day, would suddenly reveal everything about him.

The next morning, Irene gathered up the mail and took it into
the kitchen. She opened a padded, brown envelope. It contained
a glossy catalog from Gil's gallery in Santa Fe: thirty portraits
of Irene America, as well as smaller black-and-white images of
earlier portraits. There were lists of reproductions of the big
pieces. Gil's beloved doors. She had allowed him to paint her
on all fours, looking beaten once, another time snarling like a
dog and bleeding, menstruating. In other paintings she was a
goddess, breasts tipped with golden fire. Or a creature from
the Eden of this continent, covered with moss and leaves. He'd
done a series of landscapes, huge canvases vast with light, swimming Albert Bierstadt or Hudson School replicas, in which she
appeared raped, dismembered, dying of smallpox in graphic
medical detail. She had appeared under sheaves of radiance, or
emerging from the clay of rough ravines.

Irene had received other catalogs from other shows and,
always, had hastily flipped through the reproductions and set
them aside. It was best not to look too long at the paintings, best
not to examine them. She had always known that if she did, her
portrayals would stick in her mind. She would have trouble sitting naturally for her husband, she would begin to imagine or
even dread the outcome. She wanted to always be strictly in the
present when Gil painted her.

But because she knew he was reading her diary, and all the rules were broken, she looked carefully at this catalog. The new images were a mixture. Some were starkly sexual, stirringly tender. Others were such cruel portrayals that her eyes smarted and her cheeks burned as if she'd been slapped. She had a gloating, cavernous, hungry beauty in some. In others she was a guileful thing, greedy, or possessed of a devious sweetness that she found hateful. Her stomach turned over. She shut the catalog. Unsteady, she sat down and stared out the window, trying to breathe away the lurch of sickness. Suddenly she rose and went into the bathroom, opened the cabinet, swiftly uncapped a bottle of antacid, and gulped down the chalky liquid.

The image is not the person, she thought, or even the shadow of a person. So how can a person be harmed by the depiction, even appropriation, of something as intangible as one's image?

The violent physicality of her reaction confused her. She said nothing about it later, when she went to sit for a portrait, as she'd promised Gil. But a swoon of sensation invaded her as she approached the door to his studio, and she went downstairs again and had a drink, two drinks, and brought another with her, so she could ease into the session with a pleasant buzz.

They rarely talked when Irene sat for the portraits. Instead, they listened to music. But after a while the liquor wore off, Irene's head ached, and she found Joni Mitchell insufferable.

I hate that smug quality, the self-involved journey-of-life thing is what I hate, Irene said.

Should I change it?

Just turn it off. I want to talk.

All right. Just, please, don't move your head.

Paint my legs. My head's gonna move.

Gil put down his brushes. Well, it seems you don't want to sit, this isn't good, why go on working? I can quit. I've done enough.

Of all Irene's extraordinary qualities as a model, her earnest stoicism had always touched Gil most deeply. She could hold a position for a shocking amount of time, and after a break return to it as though her body remembered its precise configuration. She never complained of cold or hunger, pain or boredom. She had the patience and avidity of an artist. And he had never painted anyone who could project emotion through her flesh with such urgency. Now, though, she grudged him.

She gave a whining sigh. Go ahead. I'll talk like thith.

Gil picked up a brush; he wanted to work. She was annoying him. He leaned forward and stared intently at her without listening to what she said.

Gil, do you ever think about privacy, I mean, as a notion, how much people are entitled to it? How much people give up when they're together, say, how much privacy is important or right? Gil?

He was still staring at her, his eyes moving in tiny, sharp jabs.

Gil?

Of course I think about it. What's happened to us is wrong and disturbing.

Irene waited. Maybe he had already seen what she had written.

Gil pointed at her with the brush. Can you put your eyebrow back? Yeah. The way it was. Thanks.

So, privacy?

We are illegally spied on and wiretapped by our own government and Congress is doing nothing and people are complacent and nobody seems to give a shit that we are giving up one civil right after the other in the name of national security. Please. Just . . . yes . . . I like the way you're breathing.

Should I hold my breath, Gil, want me to hold my breath?

Yeah, and we think we're living in our regular country, but there's another country right beneath everything we do, a reflected country of war and renditions and bad secrets.

Can I let my breath out? Can you stop talking political

shit? I didn't mean privacy as in civil rights, I meant as be-tween humans in an emotional sense.

Yeah. Emotional. Fuck everyone outside Irene's drama.

You aren't listening. Irene sounded hurt.

I am. I'm sorry. I just . . .

I've been transparent to you all my life.

Gil was absorbed, looking back and forth between Irene and the canvas.

Irene stared at the beams in the ceiling. She watched a tiny pale spider descend on its silk.

I think it's the same in the personal sense. When you take away that person's privacy you can control that person.

Gil still said nothing. Irene's thoughts flickered away.

You know, Gil, we may have extraordinary children. I mean, I know, they are amazing people—Stoney is an angel, isn't he? And just wildly imaginative. Riel's got all As. Florian is a genius, probably. I wish my mother could see how they are turning out. I miss her.

I know you do, honey.

People think after a year, two years. But I miss her, Gil, right this minute. I wish I could talk to my mom.

I know, I'm sorry, it really isn't very long. Gil put down his brush and walked over to the small refrigerator. He plucked up a glass and poured from a bottle of wine. He held the glass carefully by the stem, leaning down to Irene. He set the half-full bottle next to her.

Irene took the glass. She was quiet for a time. Then she

blurted: She would not let you fuck me up like this. Winnie Jane. She didn't like you.

No, come on, Irene.

Gil kept painting.

For a while neither spoke.

I think you should see a shrink again, Gil.

You're the one who needs a shrink.

That's so true. A shrink could help me figure out why I stay with you!

Gil laughed, but now his heart began to pound and his throat stung.

Because you're crazy, Irene.

That's why I stay with you? You really think so?

Or smart. I mean, look. I love you and I love the kids. I support us. We're comfortable. Our life is successful . . . I mean, consider where we came from. You'd have to call our life, our family, a fucking miracle.

I liked my childhood.

You were carted to every AIM event. Your mom had a hundred boyfriends.

Ten.

Your dad was—

Hey, it was the times. At least I had a dad.

Mine was a—

Please don't say war hero because who knows how many Vietnamese women and children and old people your dad slaughtered, huh? You have no fucking idea, Gil.

Are we really doing this again?

Irene put her hand across her face.

Gil, I'm serious. We need some kind of help.

I don't think so. I think we're happy. I'm happy, Irene.

Gil was sweating, afraid she was going to tell him about the other man, but wanting her to tell him, too, at the same time. His head began to swim. He sat down and started cleaning his brushes.

I guess I'm done. I guess that's enough, he said at last.

Irene was asleep.

Gil shook her. He helped Irene up and she followed him down the stairs.

He had been warned about painting his wife. It would be hard on their marriage. But he'd started before they were married. Wouldn't it have been worse to stop? A rejection? And besides, even when they argued he was at peace painting Irene. She was there in front of him and he didn't have to wonder what she was doing. Besides, Hopper had painted Jo, Rembrandt had painted Saskia, then Hendrickje. Wyeth had painted Betsy and of course Helga; Bonnard had painted Marthe; there was the limitless and devouring Picasso; de Kooning and Kitaj and John Currin painted their wives. It was a way of getting at the essential other, the unknown essence, and the painting was also an act of fascinated love. Although, it was true, in the depiction of Irene, he had not always been gentle, he thought that he had used her humiliation as something larger—as *the iconic suffering of a people*, one critic had said. He hadn't dared show the article to Irene; the phrase seemed chokingly reductive.

Don't paint Indians. The subject wins. A Native painter himself had said this. You'll never be an artist. You'll be an American Indian artist. There will be a cap on your career. You'll only go so far. You'll set up expectations. Attract only one set of collectors. Look at Rauschenberg. He was Cherokee. Did he paint Indians? No. And George Morrison, the one Native artist Gil revered. He did not paint Indians. He painted their consciousness. Blacks can be postracial. But Indians are stuck in 1892. Again, Gil had no choice. He painted Indians when he painted his wife because he couldn't help it—the ferocity between them, the need. Her blood ancestors came out in Gil's paint as he worked. He developed his paintings with fanatical care—poring over the works of masters and even master forgers, who often had tricks, kitchen tips, secret mixtures, and shortcuts. He'd teased out the secrets of washed oils, black oils, hand-cooked mediums, and hand-ground pigments. Sometimes he took pleasure in working with slow applications of glaze over glaze of transparent color to achieve a slightly blurred sfumato that shook the children's sense of reality. Each of them when young had called out to the mother depicted on his canvases, and cried when she didn't answer. His technical mastery had pushed his paintings past the West and Southwest, into Los Angeles and Chicago, Philadelphia,

Washington, and then at last into New York, but he had not made the big leap. He was still classified as an American Indian artist, or a Native American artist, or a tribal artist, or a Cree artist or a mixed-blood artist or a Metis or Chippewa artist or sometimes an artist of the American West, even though he lived in Minneapolis.

A very cold winter was predicted, and it began with a surprise subzero weekend, dry and snowless. The lake froze so quickly, and on such a windy day, that the ice showed the pattern of each tiny plate as it fused with the next. Irene and Riel took their skates and went out, but never put them on because they found themselves down on their hands and knees crawling across the ice. The lake was filled with an indecipherable writing.

It seems like we should be able to read this, Riel thought, sitting back on her heels.

The lake could have written its whole life story and we'll never know it, said Irene.

They stared at the cuneiform marks and then crawled to a patch where the writing stopped, where the ice was clear and dark all the way down, like a window to another world. They lay on their stomachs and peered in, past the planar fusions and trapped bubbles of air.

I wish we'd see a fish or a turtle or something more down there, said Riel. And it did seem almost anything might swim into view. But there was only an amber leaf, a frayed heart suspended at the edge of a vertical white crack that went down so far it disappeared.

The explorer Amerigo Vespucci had signed the first map of the eastern coast and thereby accidentally named two continents and, much later, an ancestor of Irene's. America. It had been American. American Horse, a famous chief, her father had claimed. She didn't think so. She thought his name was stolen. Winnie Jane had traced American Horse's lineage and copied pictures from books, anyway. Winnie Jane's own Ojibwe family name was Sourcier, courtesy of some French voyageur, but she'd broken with her family. She wouldn't even use the name although she stuck with her clan, the crane clan, ajijak. Anyway, priests and Protestant missionaries had misunderstood the language or idea of the names and attempted rough approximations on baptismal or marriage documents. Traders had written Indian names down on notes indicating so many buffalo or beaver skins were to be surrendered for so much rum and ammunition. Guns, liquor, god, and government—the source of American Indian surnames that once were so intensely personal. Irene America. Her name was now a cipher joined to simulacra. And the portraits were everywhere. By remaining still, in one position or another, for her husband, she had released a double into the world. It was impossible, now, to withdraw that reflection. Gil owned it. He had stepped on her shadow.

Winnie Jane had once shown Irene a photograph of children attempting to extinguish a shadow by covering it with pebbles. She had told Irene of a medicine person who healed the sick with his shadow. An evil windigo warrior whose strength was in his shadow but whom a little girl was able to kill exactly at noon. A soul could be captured through a shadow. It was in the Ojibwe language. Waabaamoojichaagwaan— the word for mirror also can refer to shadow and to the soul: your soul is visible and can be seen. Gil had placed his foot on Irene's shadow when he painted her. And though she tried to pull away, it was impossible to tug that skein of darkness from under his heel.

What about my name? said Riel. Tell me about my name again.

You're named for a poet, said Irene, a poet whose visions of an Indian nation died in the bloody snow at a place called Batoche, in Canada. This is why you must be strong.

She was speaking in a dramatic voice. She smelled strongly of alcohol, dusky perfume, and a thick warmth. Her hair was snarled and sour. They were curled on the couch with the dogs' tails over them even though the dogs were not allowed on the couch. Gil walked in and the dogs jumped off. They walked around him carefully, parsing his mood. But Gil was distracted and strode quickly through the room. Stoney had tumbled into sleep on the end of the couch holding tight to his frayed lion. The dogs jumped back onto the couch and wedged their haunches between Riel and Stoney. Irene gathered Riel closer.

Louis Riel was only fighting so that Indians and Metis could have their land, said Irene. They'd been working their land for years. The government would not give title to their land. It's always the same story. Stoney was named for the great chief Stone Child called by some people Rocky Boy. I was named Irene for the song Good Night Irene, which apparently my dad heard in a bar on the night I was born. I don't think that he heard all of the words, said Irene to herself.

What words, said Riel.

The jump in a river and die words. The song is really kind of morbid, but your dad used to sing it to me and we'd laugh.

What's morbid?

Deathy.

I'm glad you love Dad so much, said Riel. I'm glad you're happy. Even if you fight, you're happy, right? I mean, people can't agree all the time, can they? So it's normal when you get mad.

Riel kept talking, faster.

I know you love him because you kiss him and I know he loves you because he paints you so much and also he tells us all of the time how much he loves you and how he would do anything for you, Mom.

Go to sleep, honey, said Irene. I'll see you in my dreams. She began to stroke Riel's forehead and Riel's eyes closed. Irene sang Good Night Irene, including the morbid words *I love Irene, God knows I do. I'll love her until the seas run dry. And if Irene won't love me, I'll take morphine and die.* She heard Gil laugh.

Who's handing out morphine? Gil walked into the room. The dogs jumped off the couch. He bent down, picked up Stoney, and carried him tenderly up the stairs.

Irene was an undisciplined reader and kept a mess of half-read books beside her bed, as well as on the coffee tables and in the bathrooms. She rarely had the patience to read one book entirely through, though she did take notes on index cards. Stacks of cards were sloppily jammed here and there, destabilizing the already collapsing piles at the bedside. Gil's reading was more careful. If he began a book, he finished it. His reverence for books had started with the cast-off marvels his mother had brought home. The smell of mildewed pages. The broken spine, torn, showing the cardboard. Nothing mattered but that the book be rescued like a human thing. Gil never laid a book on the floor. He always put a magazine, some paper, even a kitchen towel underneath so as not to scratch the cover. Therefore, the talus slopes of books on Irene's side of the bed offended him. She was a raucous, impertinent, even disrespectful reader. Gil wouldn't dream of using a Kleenex for a bookmark. He looked at splayed paperbacks with anxiety, and always fetched a strip of paper to close gently within the pages. He seemed to think he needed a bookmark at the ready when he shut his books, the way a medic has a bandage handy to staunch a wound once he lifts away direct pressure. It was as if the words would escape once Gil took his eyes off them. This was one of Gil's little habits that Irene found endearing.

Irene dipped in and out of several books at once and didn't even read research books straight through but sometimes paged first to the exciting parts, the battles or weddings or deaths. If she was about to read a biography, she opened the book at once to the photographic insert and studied the faces before she turned back to the beginning. No wonder she could not follow through and obtain her doctorate, Gil thought. How could she possibly be a scholar? Gil wondered at her lack of resolve. He felt that it was better to let a portrait of a person accrue through words, and use the photographs for reference, later on. The way Irene read often exasperated him, but he envied it in a way, too, and it was further evidence to him of her confidence with books. She treated them like servants; he *was* their servant.

Irene often told Gil anecdotes from books she was reading. Sometimes she pretended that she didn't know what book her story had come from, that she had forgotten its source. Gil liked tracking down her vignettes—holding her feet to the fire, he called it. Often, he discovered she had enlarged upon an episode in order to make some point. She didn't want him, in fact, to go back to the original text and find she had mistold the story.

Although he found this infuriating, he was captivated, too, because he believed that she was trying to communicate with him through metaphors. The night after Irene had sat for Gil, she told him she had been reading the letters and notes of the artist George Catlin.

Catlin was born in Wilkes-Barre, Pennsylvania, in 1796, the fifth of fourteen children. He was educated as a lawyer and practiced for two years before abandoning the bar in 1823 and becoming a portrait painter. In 1831 he began a series of visits to various tribes, chiefly in the Plains. He spent years among the Indians, studying their habits, learning their languages, painting them.

The story Irene told Gil was of the time George Catlin was stopped on a riverboat by Mandan people, a tribe he'd just left. They had followed him in order to retrieve the portrait of a beautiful girl. They told him that the girl, whose name was The Mink, was dying. They believed that the picture Catlin had made of her was too much like her. Catlin had put so much of her into it that when he took his painting away from their village, it drew a part of her life away with it. She had begun bleeding from the mouth. She was throwing up blood. Her family told Catlin that by taking the portrait with him he was drawing the strings out of her heart and they would soon break. They asked him to return the portrait.

But Catlin refused to give back the picture, said Irene. He said that he had also put himself into the picture by using his own spirit in the making of it. Should that picture go back, he would become ill himself.

The people offered to take the picture immediately and burn it. Such a thing that could diminish two persons really should not exist, they said, it was dangerous. Catlin said that he would burn it himself. The people went away not believing him, still in despair. By the time they returned home, The Mink was dead. Catlin exhibited her picture in Catlin's Indian Gallery in 1838, Albany, New York.

The next day, Gil found the story Irene had referenced in the second volume of *Letters and Notes on the Manners, Customs, Conditions of the North American Indians.* Letter 54. It was a story within another, longer story—sort of a lead-up, or an aside. Although the first part of Irene's version of The Mink was true, the second part was false. Catlin had actually returned the portrait. In fact, he had rolled it up and given it to the girl's people immediately, even though he didn't want to part with it. There was no way to determine from the book whether the portrait had survived or whether some copy of the portrait was made and exhibited. Gil thought that perhaps Irene was trying to tell him something by referencing and falsifying the story. Was he stealing something from her by painting her? Was he making some sort of copy of her that resided in another dimension from the paintings? Had he put so much of her into some image of her he'd created that he was weakening or diminishing the "real" Irene somehow? Was he drawing the strings out of her heart and would they soon break? Or had they already snapped?

November 6, 2007

BLUE NOTEBOOK

When I left the house this afternoon, you asked if I was going to the grocery store and I said no. But I did not offer an explanation. I simply smiled and went out the door. Why should I tell you where I am going? It is what a person does in a civilized relationship. Ours is not—you have broken the rules. Of course, as soon as I say that, I remember. I have broken other rules and you have broken other rules. We have tried to work out our differences over those violations, or over most of them. The worst things we've done have involved the children. So we have tried to repair our behavior and correct mistakes for them. But this is different.

When I picture you descending the stairs to my writing room and fishing my diary from behind the old accounts files, I feel unbearable things. I know that this is the sort of petty violation other people might get over.

But I . . .

Here, Irene stopped and wrung her dry, cold hands. She was chilled to the core and began to shake. She put her coat back on and continued.

. . . see this as a matter of life and death.

You will read what I wrote about the moment you suddenly revealed everything, the moment that I stopped loving you, the moment I understood who you really are. But there was no moment. You should know that.

How many times have I told you how difficult it is to resist the lure of the historical moment? The one action, the instantaneous truth that changes everything? How many times have I described my own struggles in telling stories, relating historical occurrences, searching for the sequence of events that results in a pattern we can recognize as history? There are always many moments, there is never just one. There are many points of clarity and many causes to one effect. However, after many, many, of these points, these moments, have occurred, there is, I should tell you, a final moment. A final scene.

With every person whom I have left, there has always been a final moment where I have realized *I am gone*. With lovers it has always occurred in the moment after my orgasm. In that stunned peace I have the certainty that I have reached the end. That we have gone as far as we can go in this life. That our lovemaking is now over. Those final moments have always occurred after the most frenzied, often desperate or furiously unrestrained lovemaking. I will touch a bruise or bite mark then and think, *you will be gone before this fades.* I will have no doubt whatsoever about this truth.

Such a moment might be captured on film, on the face of an actor. Or in a painting. You have captured it in my portraits without knowing what you've caught, I think. In a work of fiction, this particular truth would seem to me banal. But in life, it is a moment that seems weighted and graceful, though very sad, like a natural death. It is not really a moment one can act upon where there are children involved, however. One must keep trying. So although I have had many moments after sex with you in which I realized *I am gone, this is over, the end is clear*, I have been always forced to suppress an absolute awareness of finality. I cannot carry through. I go on, in other words, making love with you after the end. So many natural deaths have occurred by now I wonder how can you make love to me at all? I am a dead woman whose reflexes alone can be activated. Yet, over time, this will-less resurrection has come to possess its own dark excitement. As with those nights when I have gone to the end with others, I've ceased to care what I show of my greed. Even cruelty. And you as well. As a consequence, there is a deepening contempt in our sexuality. With the same shame I feel when I imagine you reading my diary, I admit at times I find this thrilling.

As soon as Irene came in the back door, she heard Gil charging up the basement steps. He has been in my office, she thought. He has been reading my red diary. She tore away her coat and scarf. With a savage jerk, she kicked her boots off. They hit the wall. She threw herself on the couch in the warmest corner of the living room. The dogs surged up to her. They were tense and wanted to walk. They set their heads in her lap, eyes passionately upturned. They jealously knocked each other out of the way, twisting their jaws up in pleasure when she stroked them. Suddenly she grabbed the older dog and hoisted him into her lap like a puppy. The dog squirmed like a child in alarmed delight. Though he was heavy, she tightened her arms and held the dog, whispering into his ear until he relaxed against her, lolling and quiet. After a while, Irene realized she had embarrassed her dog and let him turn over until he gave a comfortable groan. She sank her fingers into the silky tufts behind his ears and he closed his eyes. The other dog put his head on her knees and stared up at her. They were emotional savants. They knew everything.

What is going to happen? Irene whispered.

Gil spent no time wondering what he had done to make Irene fall out of love with him shortly after Stoney was born, because he knew exactly what he'd done. Stoney was born on 9/11 in a birthing room in the Riverside-Forest Hospital in Minneapolis. The room was decorated with pale green flowered wallpaper and had salmon leaping in a border. Spawning upstream, Irene said, then dying. Appropriate for a birthing room? I don't think so. She thrashed the sheets off her legs. There was an enormous television on the wall as well as a La-Z-Boy chair covered with E-Z Wipe plastic. Irene had tried to sleep the night before, but by five A.M. her contractions were keeping her awake and at seven A.M. they were checked into the room. When Irene saw the television, she said, who the hell would watch TV while giving birth? Gil had just been thinking that he might, when one of the nurses ran in and said, You've got to see this. She turned on the television. They saw the World Trade Towers collapse and Irene's labor stopped for about an hour.

You have to turn off the television now, she said to Gil, if you want me to have this baby.

But . . . said Gil.

Irene gave him a startling look of hatred. It was exactly as if she had taken a mask off. The feral rage in her expression jolted him, and after that he tried to breathe with her and time her contractions. But he also was compelled to take breaks and found himself running out to the lounge to see what was happening. Every time he tried to leave again, Irene gasped and said, Please don't go. But he did go out, over and over again, even after one of the nurses said, in a clipped voice, She needs you. They'd had to fetch him from riveting commentary for the actual birth. It was this TV-watching behavior, which he'd apologized for and abased himself for and apparently could never make up for, that Gil believed had caused Irene to fall out of love with him.

In the evening Gil turned to Irene and said, You know, I'll never forgive myself for how distracted I was when Stoney was born.

Irene didn't look at him. You've apologized enough for that, she said, does it still bother you? I've forgotten it.

Stoney sat on one end of the table with a ream of copy paper and a box of colored markers. He could draw anything. Nothing intimidated him. You want a city? Stoney drew pages of attenuated skyscrapers with tiny windows in wavering, resolute, rows. You want a herd of elephants? Buffalo? Rhinos? Birds? You want birds? Stoney could draw any kind of bird. You want the birds to ride bicycles? You want the buildings on legs? You want building-head people? You want clouds with that, or blue sky, or sun? He made drawings to order, and he made them from life. He drew his father sleeping on the couch. He drew the dogs watching him sleep. He drew Riel studying or playing World of Warcraft, which she wasn't supposed to do. Riel said to hide the drawing, and Stoney did. He drew Florian with a green bandanna, a portrait he liked. Florian showed his little brother his secret tattoo—the snake swallowing its tail. Stoney drew it, gave the drawing to him, and didn't tell anyone. He drew his mother almost every day, in beautiful dresses. He gave his mother stripes and polka dots and if he made a flowery dress he put a matching flower in her hair. In every picture, at the end of his mother's hand, Stoney drew a stick with a little half-moon on the end of it.

Before dinner, Irene was sitting with Riel and Florian. Stoney was giving an exhibition. He was showing them his stack of pictures.

Look, said Irene, when she'd paged through her portraits and admired her carefully drawn outfits. There's this thing on my hand, like another appendage, it's always there. In every picture. What is it, Stoney?

The wineglass.

Irene was silent.

He thinks it's part of you, said Florian.

On some mornings Gil went out to sit with the Lucretia. She was a five-minute drive from the house. For an hour or so after the doors opened, there were practically no people at the Minneapolis Institute of Arts. Gil said that it was like having his own Rembrandt, minus the insurance costs and the anxiety over upkeep. He knew the museum's curators—*Americas 6, 18,* and *70* were in the permanent collection. But the guards, sparse anyway, knew Gil only as the man who loved the Rembrandt. He would take his place on the wooden bench before the painting, sit with her for half an hour, or longer if nobody else came and stood between them.

Lucretia's story was told by the Roman historian Livy in *Ab Urbe Condita*. She was a devoted and virtuous wife. While her husband was away, the cruelly lustful Sextus Tarquinius tried to seduce her. When she refused him, he threatened to kill both her and his slave and leave them together in her marriage bed for her husband to find upon his return. She then gave in. Upon her husband and son's return, she told them of the rape and then stabbed herself to death in front of their eyes. Rembrandt painted Lucretia three times. One of the paintings is lost. Another depicts Lucretia just before she plunges the knife into her heart. The Lucretia in Minneapolis has already committed the violence to herself and still clutches the stained knife. Her dressing gown is soaked with blood, the gossamer clings hauntingly to her skin, her spirit dissolves her features in a muted blaze, violently alive even as she drains of life.

Gil watched Lucretia's eyes brimming with transcendent shock. Her eyes had been filling with tears since 1666. There was immense tenderness in her gaze. A sorrow that could shake Gil. Some mornings he sat on the bench and his eyes, too, welled and his vision blurred. He'd often wondered what the lost Lucretia looked like. Once, he'd painted Irene as Lucretia. In the portrait, Irene also wore a look of unutterable sadness. The look of a woman so deeply shamed, and so in love, that she could not bear to live with the stain between herself and her husband. In the painting, Irene was clothed like the Lucretia, in blood and rust. Her right hand also gripped a cord slender as the life that was left in her. But instead of a knife in Irene's other hand, Gil had painted a bottle.

Gil loved his family with a despairing sort of devotion, for he knew that on a fundamental level they shrank away from him. Their petting smiles, their compliments, their contrived laughter. Sometimes he believed they meant these things. Sometimes he knew they were afraid of him. He had hurt them all, but not really hurt them in a lasting way. He'd struck out at each of them, but he had never left a physical mark. That was important. He was taciturn, depressed, sarcastic, charming. He'd grin when Irene thought he was going to yell, turn fond on a dime. And he hadn't always been so angry. The truth was, he needed Irene's full attention. He'd had it before the children came. They took it away and he was jealous from the beginning.

He was aware of his jealousy. He knew he wanted Irene entirely. They were both raised by single mothers and their bond was deeply understood at first—they would be parents to each other as well as lovers. It had worked until they became real parents. For Irene, the love she felt for the children was a revelation. It was this way, too, for Gil, but he was also crushed because he could see that Irene now loved the children first, and she would always love them best. With each pregnancy, they touched less often, though he painted her obsessively. Gil felt the tide going out slowly, just a little every day until now he stood alone far up the dry beach.

So when he hurt them, he made up for the wrong in elaborate ways. He tried. Sometimes it twisted his heart to try, sometimes he was disappointed with the results—humiliating plans for the perfect dinner at which everyone ended up miserable, or gifts that were received with bubbly gratitude and then hidden in a closet.

Of them all, Riel was the one he found hardest to please. She seemed to want nothing. It had always been that way. When he'd asked her what she wanted for Christmas last year, she'd asked for paper. I'll give you paper, all right, he'd said. That was all she got from him that Christmas and the worst of it was he couldn't tell if she was legitimately happy when she opened the box of paper, or whether she was being sarcastic, like he himself might have been—except, he reminded himself, he too had wanted paper, endless paper to draw upon, when he was a child.

Riel stood on her box of paper to take down her secret stash of candy from the top shelf in her closet. Riel used her paper for all sorts of things. She used it for drawing endless cartoons. She made animals out of paper, glue, bottle caps. She taped leaves to paper. When she had asked for paper, there was no irony in the request. It was good to have a ready supply of paper, and she was always glad to have it when a new project occurred to her.

As she was eating Halloween candy—she was down to waxy peanut butter kisses now—Riel thought about her vampire costume, and then realized she could not remember what she'd dressed up as the year before. Then she noticed that the events of yesterday, or even that very morning, were not as vivid as the things she had done an hour ago, a moment ago, or was doing right in the present. When she tried to remember what she had done even one week ago, on the same day, that day was indistinct. Specifics were muddy. Even people. She closed her eyes to call up the face of her teacher, Mrs. Strom, and of her friends, one by one. They appeared, briefly, but like faces in a moving stream it was impossible to fix them. Their images rippled away. Even her mother's, father's, and Stoney's. But when she called up her older brother's face, she was startled at how clearly Florian showed himself. Florian steadily smiled or frowned at her. He did not disappear but on the contrary multiplied so that she could shuffle through his moods and looks as if through a pack of Florian cards.

There was Florian working, studying, his lips pressed firmly together. His pencil flew over the page as he solved arcane math problems. Florian, named for his father, Gilbert Florian, and his grandfather Florian LaRose. Riel could summon her brother shaking water out of his hair, standing lean in his ripped jeans and rock-band T-shirts—he had dozens of them. The jeans and black T-shirts were a kind of Florian uniform. The Smiths. The Kinks. Alice in Chains. The Cold War Kids. She could see him so clearly, while everyone else was bafflingly hard to fix in her thoughts. He shared this curious disparity with the dogs. She could see them at any moment, no problem. Still, the rest of it alarmed her.

Riel decided to construct a memory chart, so that she would not lose things that happened. She filled an old looseleaf binder with her special paper. She would write a memory on each page. When she recalled the memory on purpose, or it occurred to her by chance, she would enter a date. She would piece things together. She was proud of thinking of the loose leaf binder because she realized that it would probably be impossible to go through her memories in the order of occurrence. She would have to be alert and write them down whenever they showed up.

For the next few days, adding to the memory chart, she became aware of herself as an Indian, an American Indian, a

Nebraska.

Native person. Many of the events that she remembered were powwows, visits to her grandmother, wakes, moments during ceremonies, times she'd put tobacco on the ground to pray with her mother. Some of these things hadn't happened for years. But she was still an Indian. Her skin was pale, her eyes a muddy hazel, but she was still an Indian, wasn't she? She had also learned about Indians in school. She had learned that they could survive in the wild, that they lived on buffalo, hunted with bows and arrows, never cried except when looking at the ruin white people had made of their land. Indians wore powwow clothes all of the time and could talk to animals. Riel had to wonder why she couldn't do any of these things. Maybe she could train herself. It could come in very handy to be an Indian, after all.

Riel remembered Stoney's birth, the same day as the day the Twin Towers were hit. She had seen it all on TV with the stunned babysitter. After that day, she had known that anything could happen. She must be ready. She must plan how to survive a terrorist attack, using the skills of her ancestors. She looked through the piles of books at her mother's bedside for information, and took the volumes marked with green and pink slips of paper, old green hardcover books. Riel brought the books to her room and began to read them every chance she got.

She read about the burial of Chief Black Bird and his horse, high on a beautiful bluff over the Mississippi. The dead chief's

Missouri.

Black Bird was a chief of the Omaha, the upstream people

Write to Louise to correct!

hands were painted with vermilion, and his hands were pressed on the flanks of his favorite horse, the handprints to possess it forever.

Bearing the body of Chief Black Bird, who was dressed in all his finest, and who carried weapons and tobacco, the horse stood passively while earth clods and grass turfs were placed around his legs and up the sides of his body, immobilizing him so that once they reached his neck the horse was easy to bury alive.

She read about how George Catlin broke into the wild-flower-covered grave years later and stole the skull of the horse and the skull of the chief to display back east.

She read how the Mandan placed the skulls of their ancestors in circles and talked to them lovingly and spent whole afternoons in communion with their spirits, and how in the oldest of these circles the skulls had turned to chalk and disintegrated to dust so that only the teeth were left in the grass. Circles of polished teeth.

She read about Chief Mahtotohpa, a doting father and husband whose valiant and bloody life story was drawn out on a buffalo robe. Mahtotohpa's brother was killed by the warrior Wongatap and his body left with a lance sticking through it. Mahtotohpa took the lance, kept it for four years, his brother's dried blood still on it. Suddenly after four years were up, Mahtotohpa jumped up brandishing the lance and cried out, *The blade of the lance shall drink the heart's blood of Wongatap, or Mahtotohpa mingles his shadow with that of his brother!*

Mahtotohpa traveled two hundred miles to his enemy's village. As everyone prepared to sleep, he walked into his enemy's lodge and ate from a bowl of meat cooking on his fire, then, showing his face, he speared Wongatap to death and somehow escaped the outcry and chase.

She read about the sight of prairie grassfires at night, how they crept across the tops of bluffs in necklaces of liquid fire. She read how the Mandan caught horses with rope lassos and alternately choked them and revived the horses with their own breath and tamed them in only hours. She read about the interesting appearance of the Mandan, who were said by Catlin to display a peculiar ease and elegance, whose eyes were hazel, gray, and blue, and who were possessed of every color of hair, including, from infancy to adulthood, a bright silvery gray or even a glowing white.

She read about the training of young Mandan warriors, how they rode continually, hunted, fasted and thirsted, were pierced and hung from ropes. How they died into the keeping of the Great Spirit and were reborn over and over during many days of ritual torture, which they endured with pleasant smiles.

As she read this history, she decided that she would not be just a Native person, an American Indian, an Ojibwe or a Dakota or a Cree, but a person of example. She would become a girl of depth, strength, cunning, and truth. Over time, she was sure, if she observed her father closely enough, she would figure out how to get the better of him. Her basic decision was this: she would take away his power.

The day after Riel began working on her old-time Indian abilities, her father was waiting in the entryway when she came home from school. Riel stood on the mat and shook the snow off her boots.

Don't make a puddle, he said. Go outside and knock the snow off your boots before you come inside.

It was only a light snow, but it had a wet and clinging texture. It was in her hair. When she came back in, Gil swept his hand toward her to brush the snow out of her hair and she flinched.

She had promised herself never to flinch, or cower, as she'd seen Florian cower, put his hands up around his head and shrink away. But she had flinched because his hand fell out of nowhere in the sunny entryway. When she flinched, she figured out later, she made him angry because it was clear from her movement that he had struck her before. And he struck her again. She put her hand to her face and said, loudly, *Why did you do that?*

That was the first part of the plan to take away his power. Always call attention to what he did.

But he was gone before she could put the next part of her plan into action and she was afraid to run after him with her still damp boots and leave drops of water on the polished wood floor.

Which was absurd, considering the drastic nature of what she intended to do.

Some Indian, she thought, but she was only temporarily dejected. After all, she had just begun.

And perhaps she had accomplished something.

Why did you do that? followed Gil into the kitchen and as he poured the wine he felt remorse. Not true remorse, but the sort of remorse that is relieved by becoming mo-tivation for a gift. As he sat down with his glass, a sudden irresistible idea struck.

He decided that he would discover what Irene, and each of his children, even Riel, wanted most, what they coveted, what they thought they could never have. He'd unexpectedly sold a painting, just a small portrait that would bring in extra cash, and he would get these things for each of them—no matter how extravagant or difficult. He decided on a secret name for his enterprise: the heart's desire project. He wanted the fulfillment of their dreams to be a surprise.

If you could have anything, he asked each one of them in turn, anything in the world, the sky is the limit, your imagination is the limit, what would it be?

Stoney frowned and said, A cloud.

Riel was still ashamed that she had flinched. Yet even in her shame she wanted her father to think well of her choice. So she said, because she knew that above all the old Indians had wanted the best outcome for seven generations, World peace.

Florian lied and said he wanted to play hockey. Gil asked him to repeat that. Florian said it again.

What do you want, Irene, said Gil, that night.

Irene said, I want you to leave.

Gil went numb for a moment, and then laughed and said, I can't. Who would take Florian to hockey practice? It's every morning at five A.M.

Gil got a big sign for Riel that said SAY NO TO WAR IN IRAQ/N and together they put it up in the yard. As he hugged her and told her they would go to meetings together to promote peace, she was happy with herself, and proud, and also fervently wished that she did not have to act like an old-time ancestor and could instead ask for high-heeled shoes, a longboard, or maybe a real skateboard, and a helmet not with pink Hawaiian flowers on it, but a black one with a winged skull in a circle of fire.

Florian allowed Gil to buy him hundreds of dollars worth of hockey equipment but on the third morning of practice, to their mutual relief, told his father that he hated the sport.

Gil hired someone from his old St. Paul artist's days, to paint Stoney's ceiling with sky and clouds. This friend's name was Louise and she did big graphic arts jobs but had loved Gil's idea of fulfilling his younger son's dream. She came over right away.

Louise also had a connection to Irene that was unknown to Gil and, in fact, to Irene herself. Louise wasn't altogether certain about this connection either, and decided not to bring it up unless there was a private opportunity. She was hoping to talk to Irene, whom she'd never met.

While Louise was painting, Irene brought her tea.

What did you wish for, asked Louise.

Something that Gil couldn't give me, said Irene.

Two days later, Louise was finished with the clouds. She packed up her paints, rags, brushes, tarp in two large plastic totes and came downstairs. Irene was getting ready to go out. Louise had taken a bus to the house, and Irene said she'd drive her home. Louise got into the car and told her that she was going to her girlfriend Bobbi's house in south Minneapolis.

Not far from where I grew up, said Irene.

Passing the Xenon Coffee Shop, Louise asked if Irene remembered when it had been a hardware store.

The best place, said Irene. I used to walk up and down the aisle looking at the little bins of screws and bolts.

They had seven kinds of plungers, said Louise. A tiny one for the bathroom sink.

And half spheres of blue chalk.

Free paint chips and, every spring, racks of garden seeds.

Every fall we got our school supplies there.

Big Sioux rulers.

Big Chief tablets.

We should double back and have a coffee there, for old time's sake, Louise said.

Really? Would you like to? said Irene.

The Xenon Coffee Shop was a pleasant retro mishmash with Formica tables, spiky-legged chairs, harlequin light fixtures, and, on either side of a tape-patched blue plastic couch, lamps whose bases were crouching panthers of black ceramic. Louise and Irene bought lattes in tall white mugs and sat at a corner table next to a deep-silled window. Outside, the first dry snow sifted like sand, hard white in a fenced courtyard. The wind lifted the dead morning glory vines and lashed them against the panes of glass.

I don't know how you know Gil, really, said Irene. Except he says from way back.

When he had his studio in the Roberts Building, I was down the hall. Then he met you and got famous, aaaay.

Louise said that aaaay the way girls on the reservation used to, except she was just a little self-conscious, which made Irene more comfortable because it was apparent that Louise had also grown up mainly in the city. But she did not have a fake reservation accent, the kind that white people and well-educated Indians sometimes took on almost helplessly, to belong.

Do you have kids? Irene asked.

I had my son when I was sixteen. Before I knew I was a happy, well-adjusted lesbian.

So he just made it under the wire.

Louise laughed. And he's lucky because my mom raised him, too. Do you powwow dance or anything? Do your kids? You've got nice kids.

Not really, not much. How come Gil never talked about you? He's not your son's dad, is he?

Fuck, no.

They laughed, again. Louise wiped foam off the top of her lip with the base of her palm, curving her fingers over her face like a fan. She had very feminine gestures that made her seem vulnerable, girlish. Her voice was light and whispery. But she wore paint-smeared Carhartt pants and a jean jacket lined with gray wool. Her hair was cut like Patti Smith's and she wore one silver waterbird earring. Lots of eyeliner. Red lipstick. Her skin was pale but her hair was dark brown, like her eyes.

Your eyes and your hair match exactly, said Irene.

So do yours, said Louise. Are you five-eleven?

Almost. We're the same height, huh.

They stared at each other. Irene asked, So what's your girlfriend like?

Bobbi's got kids too. Three. It's good, stable, you know. We're in love, we get along. Finally.

Finally?

Yeah, I was into . . . you know. Louise went vague and looked out the window. Irene waited. Louise looked back at her and drew a deep breath. Louise didn't ask if she'd been with a woman, or was interested in women, or anything of the sort. But she looked as though she wanted to say something, and in the uncomfortable silence Irene blurted out that she had once had a girlfriend.

Oh, said Louise. Once upon a time. You're a has-be-an. Louise stared and frowned in a way that made Irene start talking.

There was way too much, Irene said, identification, too much psychic connection and all that. It felt invasive.

So you found a guy who'd keep his distance by painting you naked.

Irene said nothing, waiting for Louise to apologize, but Louise didn't seem the least bit sorry. After a while, Irene shrugged.

Not just naked. I let Gil paint me with the American flag stuck up my ass. At the time, it seemed funny.

Christ, said Louise. I didn't see that one. Did you think it was, you know, a statement?

I thought it was a brilliant metaphor, which shows you.

You must have been drunk.

Of course I was, said Irene. Are you really Gil's friend?

He called me. Louise paused. First time in ten years.

I don't get it, said Irene. He did talk about you. He'd point out your name when you had shows. But I thought we never went because you'd been his girlfriend. You never even made out with him?

Once, said Louise.

I knew it!

I think he called me because, one, he knew I could paint clouds. I had painted clouds on the ceiling of my studio, like with rococo cherubs, vault-of-heaven motifs, I'd just been to

Salzburg, and, two, I think he called me because maybe there was some sort of guilt that he'd never thrown me a bone when he got rich and famous.

This isn't much of a bone.

I don't know, said Louise. I think maybe it is. We're sitting here, you know, and um, I think I've got to ask you something. I've got to ask you your dad's name.

Irene told her.

Louise said, tense and shy, He's my dad too.

Irene put her hand to her mouth, frowning. She couldn't speak for a moment. Finally, she asked, What family are you from?

He never claimed me, said Louise, and my mom got married while she was pregnant with me. So it turned out okay. I got a nice stepdad. I'm enrolled with my mom.

Irene felt a series of expressions cross her face. Her face couldn't seem to settle on a reaction. She put her hands up to her cheeks as if to press her face into shape. I'm okay, she said. You just can't know. I mean, I grew up basically alone with my mom, except for her boyfriends. I don't have brothers or sisters.

You're kidding.

Irene raised her head. I know! An Indian with no relatives. Sad. I do have lots of cousins but I don't get together with them. My mom broke away. Things were bad for her back home. So there are pieces of family, half brothers and half sisters. I don't know them. I can't absorb this. You're my half sister.

Hey, I'll be your whole sister. That's the Indian way. It's only blood.

I'm kind of in shock. I'm just in shock. Are you in shock?

No, see, I heard about you before. I just wasn't sure.

When? So you knew?

Louise nodded. But I mean, what was I gonna say?

I guess, Irene waved her hands, overcome. Her eyes filled abruptly with tears.

Does Gil know?

I doubt it.

Don't tell him then. Would you, please, not tell him?

November 13, 2007

BLUE NOTEBOOK

I have suddenly got someone else. A sister. Someone who could perhaps be just for me, the way my mother was just for me. Someone Gil doesn't know about and whom I have first claim upon. I know I've isolated myself with just the children, with just Gil. I had friends before, but I drove them away. There was no room for them once I met Gil. The dogs are enough company for me during the days. Dogs and books, then the children when they come home. But the thought that I could have Louise to call, Louise to talk to, is such a strange thing. She is almost like another me, a twin. I wonder if other people think we look alike. I think we do look alike. Our hair is the same color, our eyes. Dark brown. Skin pale to light brown. Same complexion. Heavy lips. Same size, medium, and weight, medium. Both tall. Good cheekbones, nose. Eyes slanted, too small I always thought. But hers are nice. The eyeliner is a good touch.

Stoney ran at Irene and grabbed her around the waist. He twisted his fists in Irene's baggy shirt and started weeping with all his might. His eyes were squeezed shut and his mouth wide. His missing bottom tooth made his woe more poignant. Irene's heart squeezed. Her chest hurt. Irene bent over and held her son. With her arms locked she backed up to the living room couch and tumbled them both onto the pillows. Stoney tightened his arms around Irene, still sobbing so harshly that he couldn't form words. There was nothing to do but stroke his sun-shot hair. Soon Irene could feel the hot tears soak through her shirt.

What is it? What is it?

The crying began all over again with the same miserable force. Then Stoney quit.

I don't want to be a human, he said. His voice was passionate. I want to be a snake. I want to be a rat or spider or wolf. Maybe a cheetah.

Why? What's wrong?

It's too hard to be a human. I wish I was born a crow or a raccoon. I could be a horse. I don't want to be a human anymore.

After he considered many other animals, Stoney told her mother what had happened. That afternoon, at school, Stoney had made fun of another child. The teacher had first sharply reprimanded him, then told him that the other child was handicapped, which Stoney hadn't understood.

You made a mistake, said Irene, it's all right. You didn't mean it. Did you say you were sorry?

Yes, yes, said Stoney, crying again. His rosy face was deeply flushed. His eyelashes clumped in wet points. The skin around his eyes was puffed and tinged a delicate lavender. His sorrow entered Irene and loosened her arms and made her eyes sting. She tried to hold him, but he wrenched away and said, I don't blame you if you don't want me. I should be taken away.

Irene put her arms out again and this time Stoney flung himself upon her heart. As she held him, her thoughts spun; it took a long time for her to coax Stoney into a different frame of mind. Later on, she remembered that each of her children at the age of six were thoughtful, said startling things, and had experienced shame. Sometimes the humiliation was public, sometimes it happened at home. But the first time it occurred shame always pierced deep. The feeling was new, fresh, and terrible. It made you want to crawl out of your skin. Irene had almost forgotten what the feeling was like.

Morning. The children in school. Irene at her desk. She took out the rough, brown, recycled-paper napkin from Xenon Coffee Shop and unfolded it. She smoothed it out. Louise had printed boldly and symmetrically, as if she had taken an ar-chitectural drafting course. She had used a black fine-point marker. The block of letters and numbers indicated a stable and reliable nature. Not an impulsive person, but consider-ate. Principled. Irene's own handwriting was undisciplined, clumsy, ever changing. She examined the neat economy of Louise's address, phone number, and e-mail.

Since Louise had brought up the subject of the blood rela-tionship, she must have wanted to know Irene as a sister. She must have at least wanted to meet her. It had been such a long time since Irene had made an overture of friendship that she was not sure what was appropriate now. Would it be good to call her so soon or would Louise feel pressured? Certainly Louise now understood that Irene was not the image—either heroic or degraded—that her husband painted. But still, Louise might be disappointed when she came to know that Irene was ordinary.

Maybe it is best to be ordinary, thought Irene, right from the start. Your new sister, she thought of saying, is nobody special, or, your new sister is a fricking mess. Irene would call at a time Louise would be unlikely to answer the telephone. That way Irene could leave a message, and it would be up to Louise to give her a call, if she wanted to call, if she wanted to talk.

Or e-mail. That way Louise could pretend the message went into junk mail. If she did not want to read it. But unlike everyone else, Irene did not like to communicate by e-mail. She had stopped using it because she'd felt the dismaying urge to write too much, as in an old-fashioned letter. She'd had to tell, spill, confess, whenever she began typing.

Irene had found this out when she began communicating with her children's teachers. Endless paragraphs. Embarrassing. She'd deleted her messages and instead made face-to-face appointments. These teachers' appointments were, in fact, Irene's only reliable social outlets. She enjoyed them because she could simply sit and listen as the teachers went down lists of goals and told anecdotes about Stoney, Riel, and Florian. Gil had gone for a time, but he thought the teachers were threatened by Florian and too conventional to "get" Riel. God knows what they'll do to Stoney's natural proficiency, he worried. Irene had the teachers all to herself.

But a sister. She pictured herself with the teachers referring to *my sister Louise*, or even *Florian's Aunt Louise. Stoney's aunt. Riel has an aunt living in St. Paul. Her name is Louise.*

The day was halfway gone before Irene dialed Louise's number. Louise's voice came on: *Hi, leave me a message*—direct and simple, nothing cute. But when the beep sounded, Irene put the phone down. She went back to work and was carefully taking notes on index cards, when Louise called and asked if she'd like to go out and have what she laughingly called ladies' lunch at the hotel where she was doing some work on the walls of a fancy meeting room.

More clouds?

And sky. No cherubs, thank god.

I like that place. They give you bread with a silver tongs.

The butter comes on shaved ice.

It's nice, pricey. Can I take you?

Irene flinched at herself, flushed. She thought that she might have insulted Louise by referring to money, and thereby the difference in their financial status. But Louise seemed fine.

I'm getting paid. Don't worry. Hey, there's a powwow coming up at the kids' school. Let's go there before our lunch date.

Irene agreed. When they'd hung up, she sat back in her chair, stirred by the eager affection she'd clearly heard in Louise's voice, and anxious. Would Louise still like her once she actually spent time with her, or would she like Gil better? Everyone, eventually, seemed to like Gil better. His success attracted them. He had a graceful way of delivering a beam of forceful attention to one person. People wanted to be the object of his concentration, like Irene. He had a gift for being with people, making them feel important merely by the fact that he was present and enjoying himself. He was aware of this. Talent magnetizes people, he said. Wherever they were, it was the same. Irene had stopped traveling with Gil because she'd spend her time alone, or at best in some corner with another shy worshipper of Gil. Women. He knew exactly what to notice about them. He'd learned how to make his mother happy, a giant task. Other women, he said, were a picnic. Easy. Irene had agreed that he was a great woman-pleaser. It was hard for her to understand why, when he had so many friends, when so many women might adore him, he still seemed to prefer her.

She didn't understand it was because she did not require to be pleased. In fact, she hated to be pleased, she feared it, and in the end she refused to be pleased. There was nothing Gil could do. Yet he was compelled to bring her flowers and pick out clothing and bake fresh scones for her and buy notebooks and sealing wax and refrigerator magnets and tiny flower vases and the latest celebrity-endorsed or lavish perfume. His earliest training had been to please women, so he was forced to continue in his attempts with Irene, even though the odds, as the years went on, were not just against him, or impossible, but actually made things worse.

I want you to stop giving me presents, Irene said. It is confusing. I told you to leave, and instead you give me presents.

Maybe you'll stay with me if you open this one, said Gil. He gave her a disarming smile. It means nothing. I just found it. You'll be happy that you opened it. Really, it is very small.

In the package was a delicate golden arrow, a lapel pin.

I don't like gold, said Irene, handing the pin back. No presents.

Would you like it in silver?

Really, said Irene. No gifts. She was surprised at how deeply her insistence upset Gil.

He paced the floor with the pretty box in his hand, opening it and shutting it. He saw her response as a rejection of that gift in particular and maybe of everything he stood for and all that he could do.

If you didn't want gifts, you should not have opened the box!

Gil threw the box at her face. The corner hit her cheek and Irene jumped up and grabbed a heavy brown pottery lamp, ripping the cord from the wall with a sparking crack. She had learned that Gil's first aggressive act had to be countered big; she had to scare him or he would gain confidence and really hurt her. She gripped the lamp hard at its neck, like a club, and held it cocked at her shoulder. The lamp shade clattered off onto the coffee table and then toppled silently onto the carpet. Gil's eyes flickered, and his gaze fell before her.

Stoney stood in the doorway to Florian's bedroom, watching Florian at his computer. He was clutching *The Runaway Bunny* in one hand and his lion was stuffed under his arm.

What's up, Charm Quark? said Florian. His eyes never left the screen.

Stoney climbed onto Florian's unmade bed and nestled into the pillows. He had learned that if he kept quiet, read his book, held his lion, Florian would let him stay in his bed. He wouldn't even mind if Stoney fell asleep there.

Stoney woke in the dark next to Florian. For a moment, he was so happy that he tried to keep himself awake in order to feel his own happiness. Florian's steady breathing and warm weight were a barrier to the hovering, shifting, shape-less dark. Stoney grew drowsy, but then he heard, again, the sounds that had awakened him. His mother and father were having a fight. It wasn't too bad, just yelling. No bangs, no crashes, no screams. Still, those often came. He squeezed his eyes shut. Riel crossed the hallway, closed the door against the sounds, and crept in too. Stoney reached his hand out and Riel grabbed it. Then Stoney felt all right again. Florian curled around him on the other side, a pillow crushed against his ears.

Stoney woke up just before dawn, crept silently back to his own room, and slipped between his cold sheets. He fell back asleep—no bad dreams. A little later, his mother woke him up and set out his clothing. He got dressed, still sleepy, and followed Florian down the stairs. Riel was last and hardly got any breakfast. Their bus came and took them away to school.

In the daylight the children never mentioned sleeping in Florian's bed, or holding one another's hands.

Gil was working out the paintings, the colors, the emotion, and as he did he was happy. He did not feel alone when he was working. Even when things weren't going so well otherwise, he could paint. It didn't even matter if Irene was angry. In fact, it was better. When they were happy, when he could count on her quotidian devotion, the paintings seemed to veer into insipidity. He had to wrestle with contentment. As she moved away from him emotionally, the paintings grew fiercer. They came alive with longing. He painted his pain, her elusiveness, his grasping clutch, her rejection, his bitter hope, her sullen rage into the pictures. He'd become aware that the worse things were between them, the better his work came out. It did not yet occur to him to wonder whether his suspicions about Irene were also a method of pushing her away from him, so that he could feel her absence, and in turn feel an aching desire out of which he could make his art.

Lead white, cremnitz white, ceruse, lead carbonate—this was the best white, the only white Gil would use and the most ancient of colors. Pliny had written of lead white, used for painting ships. The Romans had made it by covering lead plates with dung or urine and scraping the white flakes that formed on the lead off into jars. The Dutch masters had invented the stack process—coils of lead placed in earthen pots on stacks of horse manure in a small tight shed. Gil feared that lead white might become difficult to obtain because it had toxic properties. So he bought extra lead white when he could afford to and built up a stash in his studio closet. He slowly added to his cache the most important colors, the Velázquez vocabulary: yellow ocher and lead tin yellow, vermilion, red earth, red lake, azurite, ultramarine (the real stuff, made from crushed lapis lazuli), smalt (ground glass, a dark blue), and brown earth. When deep in a painting, he sometimes mulled his own paints, long paints that flowed in the direction of the brushstrokes. So he kept jars of ground pigments and linseed oil in his closet, too. He also had extra brushes: sable, badger, fitch, squirrel. He kept plastic bottles of baby oil and Dr. Bronner's soap to clean his hands with, as well as a few quarts of vodka in case he ran out downstairs.

His closet was extremely neat, obsessively organized. His studio was a flamboyant mess.

Some of Gil's best childhood memories were of his father's funeral. Because Gil's father hadn't married Gil's mother, who was white, or had a chance to place his name on Gil's birth certificate, Gil could not be enrolled in his tribe, which at any rate suffered termination and reinstatement, hopelessly snarling the enrollment records. Few people had even registered that the United States had troops in Vietnam when Gil's father was shipped home from there for burial. A car with brown people suddenly appeared in the parking lot of the apartment building where Gil lived with his mother in Billings, Montana. They joined the people in the car for a long ride. At last a gravel road led into rounded hills. Gil had got out of the car in a bright wind and walked into a brown shingle church with a white steeple. People were sitting here and there in the pews. There was a coffin at the front of the church, closed. An American flag was draped over the coffin and soldiers stood guard at either side.

When Gil walked up to the coffin and put his hand on the flag, a murmur began in the church. People made sounds of interest, sympathy, excitement. They came up to him, shook his hand, touched his hair, and spoke to him softly. Some of them had tears in their eyes, and they looked at one another, nodded, looked back at Gil. The old people talked about him in their own language, and Gil sensed that what they were saying was good. Later, in a small back room, they fed him meat soup and potatoes, and an old woman clung to his hand. He did not know where his mother had gone. He didn't care. He wanted to stay where he was.

They spent the night in sleeping bags, on the floor of someone's house. It was November, and the next day, when they buried his father, the wind, which had blown harshly all morning, died down and the sun blazed out from under slate blue snow clouds. From a nearby hill a man's voice rose in a chilling song and the priest fell silent. The old woman who had held Gil's hand bent over and took an eagle-feather warbonnet from a beat-up cardboard suitcase. She spoke to Gil and put the warbonnet on his head. The song went up again. Before this time, the only Indians Gil ever knew were quiet women in the grocery stores, who appeared and disappeared in the aisles, an occasional drunk person on the sidewalk, classmates with whom he did not associate, or an Indian on TV.

He felt like he was in a dream and that his life up until that moment had been false. However, once he returned home, he put the warbonnet away in the suitcase under his bed and forgot about what had happened on the hill. He didn't think of it again until he went to college on scholarship in Chicago. Finding that he was from Montana, a boy asked if he knew any Indians, and to his own surprise Gil said, My father.

Irene had told Gil that he couldn't relate to Florian because he hadn't really known his father—Gilbert Florian. Gilbert Florian LaRose. You're clearly not Dad material, Irene had said. Your mother spoiled you for being a father. Gil thought he was adequate father material, imperfect, volatile, but loving. He certainly loved his son. However, Florian had never liked him, even from the beginning. There was no spontaneous hugging and as a toddler Florian had run away from him—always toward Irene.

Now, at thirteen, Florian was tall and thin, with brown ottery thick hair that grew all in one direction, like a pelt. His face narrowed to an elegant, slightly jutting chin. His clever mouth was indented at each corner so he always seemed to be holding back a mocking smile. He had Gil's powerful, perfect nose. His cheeks were still fine and girlish. Surprisingly in a boy so handsome, he could also seem a little goofy, bewildered, his glasses tilted or slipping. One of Florian's habitual gestures was to fiercely force his black, thin-framed eyeglasses back to the bridge of his nose and hold them, staring forward, almost cross-eyed, frowning in concentration.

Sometimes, when his glasses slipped, Gil would push them back with a painful jab of his finger.

I am going to staple them to your head, Gil said to Florian once.

Irene was sitting next to Gil. She heard what he said. Florian looked at her. She was staring at nothing with a glass of wine in her hand. Florian would remember that moment. The first time he realized that his mother was drunk.

Florian had been so attached to Irene that he had wept, every day for a month, when leaving for nursery school. He had wept until he found his second love—fractals. Irene had found him examining the picture of a snowflake on the cover of a book. He took the book to bed with him. She would find him staring at stains, ferns, blots, swirls of dirt. Staring with a blind absorption at something she could not see. In their favorite music store, she picked out a CD with a beautiful and complex shape on its cover, and when Florian saw it in the car he got excited and begged until she put the CD case into his hands. The cover credits said Mandelbrot set and once she looked it up, she understood that Florian's fascination had a name. But she was also a little spooked. In everything around him, Florian had been seeking fractal self-similarity.

Irene began to look for shapes all of whose parts were reduced-size copies of the whole. Gil was the one who could really see them. He said that Jackson Pollock's paintings some times included fractal-like areas, and he picked up a branch of imitation coral in a fish store and showed her why that was a fractal. But Florian's fascination was just a prelude to what hit him when he started counting. Nobody taught him to count. His lips just started moving. He sucked up numbers. Gil bought him a box of Cuisenaire rods. Florian took the box to bed with him and got up early to sit in his rumpled bedclothes combining and recombining the different lengths and colors into mathematical calculations.

So Florian was in love with math. In fifth grade he'd finished high school math and now he went to the University of Minnesota every afternoon. He spent his mornings at the same school Riel and Stoney went to, a private school where the CEOs of seed and cereal companies, the Target executives, the semifamous—the city's star athletes, symphony conductors and doctors and lawyers—sent their children.

Irene wanted Florian to be grounded in the humanities, but he'd sneaked in a theoretical physics course and it was during that high school physics course, taught by a calm, tall, serious young black woman, that Florian fell in love once again—with his teacher, Mrs. Francine Blithe, and with physics.

Whenever Gil introduced Florian, he said, This is my son, he's a math genius. Ask him any question you like. Florian would flush and duck his head, shove his hands in his pockets. He edged out from under the weight of his father's arm. But he'd come to love the pride in his father's voice. Once, Gil had turned and looked into Florian's eyes and said, with moving sincerity, Do you know how special you are? Gil shook his son, almost violently. Really, do you know how special? Do you? Do you?

None of this would have happened if Gil had not saved Florian's life. When Florian was four years old, sitting in his car seat in the back of the car, he threw a Koosh ball at his father's head. Gil had just yelled at Florian to stop whining and Irene had reached back and given Florian the toy, a wobbly ball that looked like a fluorescent sea urchin with rubbery spines. The three were traveling south on 35W toward crosstown 62 when Florian threw the ball, which may not have caused the accident, but which Florian always remembered throwing just before Gil violently rear-ended a delivery truck. The car spun to the right shoulder and the doors flew open. Irene's air bag stayed inflated but Gil's instantly subsided. Gil turned to see if Florian was all right and saw that he had wiggled from his car seat, jumped out the open door, and was now running straight into five lanes of traffic. Gil plunged after him. There was no thought, no hesitation. His eyes were on his son. He scooped Florian up in the fourth lane and dodged, sprinted, dived, across the last one. Half-stunned, Irene edged out from under the bag and then faced the impossible flow of cars and trucks into which her son and husband had disappeared. The two of them were already across, standing in the littered median. Gil was beginning to shake. At odd times, for the next couple of weeks, he'd find himself shaking uncontrollably. He experienced a reverse dread that also stirred him when this happened. He kept thinking of the ultimate moment, the Lord Jim moment. With one act a character makes or breaks himself. He had no memory of the moment before he'd run into traffic. If he'd stopped to think . . . he quailed. But he hadn't. He'd gone right through. In seconds, they were safe on the other side. And Irene had seen it. She stood next to the car, barely able to support herself. Her hands were pressed over her mouth. Her eyes were streaming. Once it was all done and they were safe at home in bed, all three of them, and Riel, who thank god had been with the babysitter, Irene had this thought: *a life for a life*. No matter what Gil did, he'd saved her child, and they were thus sealed life to life in a primitive bond, which, however, it would take a surprisingly short time to erode.

A lifetime of forgiveness would not be enough, she sometimes thought, so why can't I stand him?

The night after Irene made the plan to see Louise, there was an opening party for a museum show—a famous artist at the Walker. Gil coaxed Irene into going. She smoothed a pearly opalescent color on her eyelids, wore a shimmering lipstick, put faint glitter on her cheeks, and tugged on a tight-fitting ivory dress, ivory stockings, and pale green leather boots with curved black heels.

Gil had bought these boots for her and, when she walked

down the steps, he stood at the bottom with his hand dramatically outstretched. He said, I will be with the most beautiful woman in the room!

Florian and Riel were standing in the entryway, and they nudged each other when their father said this. Gil said this every time he took Irene to a party. The words had been a joke to their children at first. The two still rolled their eyes, pretended to have trouble keeping straight faces. But the words had gained a certain poignancy. Florian and Riel had drifted into the entry without admitting they were waiting for the phrase. It would have distressed them not to hear it.

Because of the America portraits, Irene felt that her presence was embarrassing to other Indians, especially older people. Yet to non-Indian people in the art world, her marriage to Gil had become known as an iconic marriage. A sexy marriage. That night she heard such things said. You two are icons! Since she'd seen the catalog of Gil's show, she could not help remember that the man who said this had seen her utterly exposed, through Gil's eyes. You were clearly meant for each other, said an overdieted blond woman. He adores you, said another. You're so fortunate to have this talented husband who is obsessed with you! You two are the same kind of person, aren't you!

No, said Irene, at last, I'm just food.

What kind of food? The woman's eyes widened in fake goodwill.

Fast food, said Irene.

They both laughed, as though Irene had said something supremely clever, and then the woman turned quickly away.

Gil had grown up on Reader's Digest condensed versions of novels, and on paperback thrillers. He still loved sitcoms. Irene had grown up on Shakespeare. It seemed snobbish of her to care about it. But she did, sometimes, when people said they were alike. No, we're not alike, she would answer. We have entirely different sensibilities. *Of course you do.* The person would smile as if to encourage Irene in the fantasy that she was separate in some way from her husband. But she was. She, too, had been an only child, but a carefully reared middle-class one. Her mother made their living teaching English classes all over the city. Winnie Jane was a homeschooler, an AIM activist, a cere-monialist, a keeper of journals, and gravely thoughtful. Winnie Jane had raised her daughter as Ojibwe after her separation from Calvin American Horse. Irene hadn't seen her father for years. He traveled constantly, giving lectures, holding ceremonies. He was part Dakota and had spent time in prison after Wounded Knee. He had left Winnie Jane after a few months, married two times, had other children, including of course Louise. He mostly lived in California and Hawaii, with his current wife, a white woman, very rigid in her pagan ideology, who did not like the paintings of Irene.

Winnie Jane had lived to raise Irene and to see her grandchildren—that was something. Not enough, but something. Irene had grown up in the middle of Minneapolis without a television. Her mother had dragged her to everything Ojibwe. She learned the histories of the reservations before she had learned the Pledge of Allegiance. Winnie Jane also loved recordings of Shakespeare's history plays, and *Hamlet*, *Macbeth*, *King Lear*. None of the comedies, of course. They were Indians.

Gil had grown up watching the TV set his mother had brought home from the church basement. He could quote plots and lines from *The Brady Bunch*, *The Courtship of Eddie's Father*, *The Mary Tyler Moore Show*, *All in the Family*, and *I Love Lucy* reruns. Each episode was full of snappy comebacks, laugh tracks, an ooh-aah ending. Her endings were of course insane bloodbaths. His outlook was sentimental while hers was tragic. The union of the tragic and the sentimental is kitsch. Irene felt that whenever she opened her mouth to appreciate her marriage in public, she was giving tongue to kitsch.

They were cooking together: Irene was mixing up a vinaigrette and Gil was grinding fresh basil with olive oil and garlic.

I can't go to parties anymore, said Irene. Her voice was firm, complacent. I feel like I'm being eaten alive.

What a kitschy thing to say, said Gil. Eaten alive.

I need a clove of garlic. Can you crush a clove for me? I'll have to talk about our marriage, said Irene. I can't do that anymore.

There's not much garlic. Here. Gil scraped a bit of garlic into the jar she was using for the salad dressing. Why can't you talk about our marriage?

Because our marriage is kitsch.

Everything is kitsch, said Gil. He always dipped his lasagna noodles in hot water to soften them, which Irene said was unnecessary.

They reverted to one of their endless arguments, first about the noodles, then about kitsch. This was not fighting, but the sort of argument that could go on for years and years, where each found bits of evidence to prove their point and dropped it into the next go-round a month, two or three months, on. They were back in old territory. They argued sometimes for comfort.

All images are spoken for, said Gil. He dropped the noodles defiantly into the hot, salted, oily water.

I need more garlic than that, said Irene. Gil obligingly began to peel the last clove.

That's the problem of painting; it's all reference, he said as he inserted the peeled clove into the crusher. It is almost impossible not to make kitsch, Irene, but if you love painting, you paint anyway. I take the chance! The female nude is kitsch. You're kitsch! He opened his eyes wide at Irene as he lifted his arm and crushed the clove with a one-handed squeeze.

Gil held the garlic crusher over the dressing again, and this time Irene scraped the garlic bits away.

What's kitsch is Indians, said Irene, as images. There is no way around it. We'll never get the franchise back. She put her hand over the opening of the jar and shook the dressing.

All right then, said Gil, let's just say I am making up for the lack of kitsch in our original cultures.

Who's to say there wasn't kitsch?

Gil was smoothing a jar of tomato sauce onto the bottom layer of his noodles. He did this with painstaking thoroughness, taking care to cover every bit of the pasta.

Kitsch, he sighed, arrives only with a consumer culture and an iconic religion, a depictive religion. Irene, you should know this. You get sentiment only when a whole culture participates in a lie.

Irene shook a mixture of leaves in a zebrawood bowl, one she'd bought at a kitchen store and was proud of having. She was piqued by Gil's tone, a superiority that he always eventually assumed when talking about his art theories. He hadn't an ounce of humility, she said, or only false humility, which he showed when interviewed.

There was kitsch in Mayan culture, she went on, Inka,

Aztec. Those outtasight headdresses! Mass death. Ripping the living hearts from people. Certainly there was kitsch in those cultures—otherwise Mel Gibson could not have made a movie.

Gil screwed up his face and perched his glasses on his nose. Kitsch only happens when a culture reaches a level of self-hatred. The culture has to be self-referential. They have to have mirrors.

Bullshit. Mirrors. All I know is you're making kitsch out of me.

No, Irene. I'm painting death.

Irene raised her eyebrows and stopped talking.

But later, when they came back to finish the salad and take the lasagna from the oven: Ha, Gil, death is kitsch too.

Death cannot be kitsch.

Death is a snappy comeback, a neat ending. And it has theme music.

So you see, just as I said, everything is kitsch.

I don't want our marriage to be kitsch, though. I want to be authentic. Real.

They were carrying the food out to the table. The children were talking upstairs, ready to come down to dinner.

Reality is bad taste, said Gil. Do you want croutons?

The cornmeal ones. I love those. Kitsch is more than bad taste, Gil, it's hypocrisy. I'm serious now. It's representing something as strong and cute and unified when it is fractured and hurting and sick. Like us.

Gil had nearly left the room, but he turned back.

Like us, Irene repeated.

I think we're beautiful, Gil said, his hand on the door frame. His voice was sad and dignified. I think we're imperfect, but extraordinary. You don't know what you have in so many ways.

Gil had completed the heart's desire project, except for Irene's wish—he really would not believe she meant it, although he'd known it was coming, her asking him to leave. No chance. His art was haunted by tragedy, but his life was not; he would not let it be. No sad ending. No other man would have Irene. Instead of leaving, he was planning a wonderful surprise. Irene didn't like parties anymore? He'd change her mind! Surely, if he gave a marvelous, superlative, lavish party for Irene, she would realize at some point during the happy whirl that nobody else would have a party just for her. Nobody loved her this way. Nobody celebrated her. The moment would come. The bulb would light up over Irene's head. I really love Gil! His belief in these life-changing moments of self-realization was another thing they argued about. But he knew he was right. These moments happened. He was sure they existed. Gil clung to an obtuse innocence.

Some call this denial. People joke about denial, or even look down on those who stubbornly clutch a hopeless idea, especially when it involves a relationship. However, denial can be seen as noble in some people. It can be seen as a form of sacred craziness. Are your fingertips sensitive enough to feel a hair through a piece of paper? How about a dozen pieces of paper? Two dozen? There are people so sensitive that they can trace a hair beneath three dozen pieces of paper. Gil had that kind of sensitivity. The hair beneath the thicknesses of paper was something terrible he did not want to feel—shame, perhaps, shame, probably. No matter how much paper he piled up, he could still feel the hair. He had to work at his denial constantly, he had to keep the paper neatly piled.

He scheduled Irene's party for the evening he'd told her he was leaving for Washington, D.C., to accept an award and make a speech. On that evening, he had really invited all of the people he liked in the Cities to come over for a champagne supper to celebrate Irene's birthday. The celebration would be elegant, festive, and full of candlelight.

He thought of calling Germaine, actually calling him to invite him to the party. And maybe, before that, catching the two of them together.

Whenever Gil remembered that Irene had asked him to leave, his hurt thoughts veered to the party. What a picture: People milling around the house. His portraits of Irene on the walls. Some of the new ones. He would invite his collectors in the area, of course. This would also function as an intimate *vernissage*. Perhaps a sale or two would result. What harm in that? But he wouldn't let people into his studio, he decided. For one thing, it was a worse mess than usual. Also, he was feeling territorial. He wanted to conceal the painting he was having trouble with, the portrait of Irene he was working on now. The picture was disturbing. The energy fueled by his longing seemed to have turned negative. No matter what he tried, how he changed it, Irene looked dead.

Of course, that made the painting interesting, too.

This surprise party would lift their spirits. He was careful not to tell the children. They might inadvertently let on. He'd hired a caterer, though he'd have preferred to cook for everyone himself. He'd called Louise and arranged for her to ask Irene to lunch and then, wherever Irene went afterward, follow her, figure out how to run into her and get her home. Later, he'd question Louise about exactly where Irene had gone. By the time the party started, he'd know.

In the afternoon, while Louise diverted Irene, the caterers and Gil would rush in and set things up. All the time, Irene would think Gil was at the airport or en route to Washington. He kept imagining her face when she walked in the door with Louise. She would have seen her lover that after-

noon. Louise would tell him where. Irene would wonder if
he knew. Would she be gratified? Delighted? Horrified that
he had caught her?

November 16, 2007

RED DIARY

S ometimes I take the children over to Pow-
derhorn to see the small white house where I
grew up. We park on Longfellow and stand on the
sidewalk across from the house, looking closely at
the windows. We have never seen anyone home.
When we were there last, the yard was cluttered
with hula hoops, a scooter, and bright, plastic toys.
I would have liked that. My mother kept our life
too neat.

Gil is being given an award by an association that
represents socially progressive causes that benefit
children. He's donated paintings and done some
graphic work for this organization. It's apparently a
big deal.

It has been months since the day Gil confronted me about seeing someone else. He must have suspected it for a long time because he had gathered ideas, certainties. I wouldn't have the time for an affair, I said, and I think I laughed. I spoke the truth. There was no affair. I am faithful to Gil for the obvious reasons.

The temperature was going to drop again over the weekend, and snow would grain the surface of the ice. The rink had just been flooded. The surface was a glossy blue-gray. Irene took Stoney and Riel skating on Saturday. This was going to be a good year for skating—thick ice ever since the first freeze. Irene brought a small plastic chair in the car, for Stoney to push while he learned to keep his balance. At the skating rink, Stoney walked behind the chair with clomping skate-steps. He was avid, but careful. He was wearing a red snowsuit and a yellow fleece jester's cap with bells.

Riel and Irene skated in slow circles around the jingling Stoney, pretending to be doubles champions. Irene lifted Riel off the ice when they spun. There was an orange cone at one end of the rink, always in the same place. There, a spring came up under the ice and weakened it.

What did the old-time Indians do if they fell through the ice? Riel asked as she skated holding hands with her mother. They steered around the orange cone.

You could drive a truck over this ice, said Irene.

You always say that, said Riel. But what did they do?

They never fell through the ice, said Irene. There are many kinds of ice and they could look at the ice and they could tell immediately whether it would hold their weight.

How did they learn? said Riel.

From each other, said Irene. Knowledge passed through the generations.

Riel took her mother's arm and looked into her face. Irene smiled down at her. They got lost in each other sometimes. Riel wore a blue parka printed with snowflakes. Her brown hair was clipped short. She'd wanted to look like Florian, but her hair was so fine that when she removed her winter hat it stood out like electrified floss. From now on, she'd decided to let it grow long so that she could put it into braids.

Could you save me if I fell in? said Riel.

I could save anyone, said Irene. I would throw myself flat down on the ice and grab your hands. Or I would plunge beneath the ice to pull you out.

Could you teach me about the ice? said Riel.

If you feel the ice give, retreat! Go back the way you came, said Irene. If you fall in, throw both arms up on the ice, then try and kick up your legs.

They crossed arms, held hands, and glided with slow steps, in unison. Irene asked what Riel was doing in school.

Writing stories, Riel said.

Will somebody fall through the ice in your story at school?

I only write real stories, Riel said. I stick to exactly the way things happen. If I imagine a weird thing, I write it under Unreal Thoughts.

Like what?

Like over there, living with the dogs on that island like a real Indian, surviving a terrorist attack.

They stopped and stood together, gazing at the wild tree-covered island in the middle of the lake.

Don't forget to bring matches, said Irene, so you can start a fire.

The old-time Indians could start a fire with their bare hands, probably.

The gete-Anishinaabeg, that's what they are called. No, they used two sticks, or a flint, or a striker; they had all kinds of ways. But a match works best. If you want them to be waterproof, you dip them in wax.

Can we dip some matches into wax? Irene said yes. Riel breathed out in happiness. Her front teeth were new, outsized, rabbity. Irene smiled down at her and said, I love your teeth.

Riel looked up at her mother and right then she put her mother's face into her memory: hair in lank strings, eyes shining, white grin, black knitted cap, eyebrows long and dramatic, curving past her eyes to her temples.

Let's go fishing in the summer, said Riel. Or through the ice. You can drill down. Riel pointed at a couple of ice fishermen kneeling over their lines. From that distance, against the white snow, the fishermen looked like two people huddled in prayer. See them? Riel asked. I could cook the fish and share it with the dogs.

I think you'd better pick summer to live out there, Irene said. You've got a better chance of catching fish, and besides, it's too easy for other people to walk across the ice to the island right now. You'd want privacy. You'd want to really be alone.

Riel nodded. I wish I could take you.

Why can't I go?

You have to take care of Stoney.

When Riel said this, Irene's heart pinched. Her mother had been distant, sometimes cold, but she'd never had to share her.

Stoney called for help. Tired, he sat in the chair and Irene pushed him back and forth across the ice. Riel went off by herself, to practice twirls. The city lights reflected up into the low sky and the flossy clouds flared a deep orange. Irene had skated all winter as a child, when the skating season always seemed much longer. She kept all of the skates sharpened and waited for the good days when the ice was not too soft or the wind too harsh. She always thought while skating—

the repetitive smooth movement made her reflective. Stoney was content in the chair. Riel kept working on her turns. Irene's thoughts turned toward home. She thought of Gil, and wondered if at this moment he was reading her diary, and whether he would believe she had always been faithful.

He smelled like some kind of wet spice. He was very strong the way she was, not obviously muscular, but he could pick her up. He was taller, and moved with a slow ease, and he was kind. Irene didn't have the feeling that they were doing something wrong. They were doing what was inevitable. After making love, they'd been shaken by their comfort with each other. They could not break the grip of it. He'd missed his flight. He wanted to continue, to see Irene again. But it was immediately clear to her that they should return to their own difficult lives and pretend that nothing had happened.

For weeks Irene had thrown up every morning when she woke and realized she could not see Germaine. There were reasons. Irene was positive that this kind of true joy was dangerous and would destroy her children. If she were to continue an affair, she also saw that she would never leave Gil. The guilt would function as glue.

People rarely manage to pretend that nothing has happened in such a case, but Irene had a surprising amount of self-discipline in this area. She walled off that time with Germaine. She did not ever, or almost ever, go behind that wall. Because there had been a sacrifice involved and she had never again spoken with Germaine, she did not consider what had happened an infidelity. No, that was when you actively sought sex with another person and deceived your spouse over a period of time, wasn't it? Irene could not bear for one slipup to count, so she had simply discarded the truth. History is two things, after all. To have meaning, history must consist of both occurrence and narrative. If she never told, if he never told, if the two of them never talked about it, there was no narrative. So the act, though it had occurred, was meaningless. It did not count as infidelity. It did not count at all.

Do you have any idea what this is? Gil waved a piece of paper at her from across the room. Do you know?

Florian was sitting at the dining room table with his head down. His hands were folded over the back of his head and his shoulders were shaking.

Stoney, said Irene, go upstairs. Right now. Riel was at her afterschool Spanish class. Good.

Stoney took off like a rabbit. He sprang up the steps. He knew when to get away from things and where to go. He ran to his room and covered himself with his stuffed animals. The dogs stood near Florian, ears pricked, listening hard to the tones in their people's voices.

Whatever it is, said Irene, it will be okay.

Oh, really? This is a note, Irene, a note.

All right, Irene said, walking forward to Florian. Let me see it.

Oh, you'll see it all right, you'll see it!

Gil crumpled up the note and smashed it, hard, on the back of Florian's head. Florian's forehead hit the table with a loud crack.

Irene stepped between the two, and Gil backed away.

Give me the note, she said to Gil. Florian, you go upstairs now.

The dogs stood ready at either side of the table. When Florian jumped up, Gil strode powerfully around one side with his fist cocked and a dog bumbled into his path. Gil swung a chair at the dog and Florian ran past, up the stairs.

Sit down, said Irene. With Florian out of the room, she could work on Gil. Sit down, Gil. Let me see the note. Whatever it is, it's okay.

Gil sat down at the table and then slumped back in the

chair, his mouth slowly opening. He put out his arm and the piece of paper uncrumpled as he opened his hand. Irene took the note, smoothed it out, and read that Florian had an overdue book report and that his grade would go down one point for every day it continued to be late.

It's not so bad, she said.

It's not just the book report, said Gil.

The dogs had vanished.

It's the deception over the book report.

Gil's voice was reasonable. He'd lost his anger suddenly. His face was clear.

Florian told me yesterday he'd turned in the book report, said Gil. He lied to my face. He told me a bold-faced lie. Is this really the sort of child we want to raise?

Florian's a good boy; he's brilliant—he's just lost in other thoughts. He lied because he's scared of you, Gil.

You were not there. Gil was crisp and firm. You did not have Florian look you in the face and tell you an absolute lie, Irene. The book was sitting in the room. I said, Have you read the book? I pointed at the book. *Lord of the Flies*. I said, Is your book report done? Yes, Florian said, yes, Dad, it is done.

Well, no wonder. *Lord of the Flies*! I think—

You think. You weren't the one lied to. Don't excuse him. Don't let him get away with this. Don't be soft on him. You're too lenient. You grew up in chaos. You escaped. Not everyone is as strong as you, Irene. We can't let Florian think it is all right to lie, can we?

Let's take a minute, Irene said. She put her hand on Gil's shoulder. He slumped a little. She spoke evenly. Gil, I think Florian's working on the book report right now. I'm sure of it. Now, come on, let's you and me sit down in the kitchen and drink a glass of wine. Let's just take this chance to talk. I haven't seen you all day. What did you work on? Who called?

Who called? Oh my god, you'll never believe who called.

I don't know. Wait. Stasia?

Yes, and she loved the painting.

Really.

Loved it.

Tell me.

Irene pulled Gil upright and spoke calmly, looking into his eyes. No. Go back. Tell me just exactly what she said, in her words.

Gil's face lighted, and he spoke.

Stasia said she'd looked at it and felt the hair rise on the back of her neck. Electrified, that's what she was. She had to answer calls and so on, but all day she kept sneaking back, to the back room of the gallery, her office. She had to keep looking at it. You know the feeling.

Of course.

They walked into the kitchen, and Gil poured wine for the two of them. Irene drank hers like water and Gil refilled her glass.

Guess what happened then! Gil laughed. Later that afternoon, she canceled, actually canceled, an engagement for drinks with another artist. Why? Because she knows who wants the painting. I don't know who the other painter was. I couldn't pry it out of her. But I think this is a good sign.

It is.

A really good sign.

He didn't have time to read my diary, thought Irene. He must not have read it yet or he'd surely have tried to keep his temper, wouldn't he? The faithfulness, that would have appeased him. That would have put him in a good mood, wouldn't it?

I worked straight through, said Gil. I'm just wiped out.

What's on the news?

I'll check. Let's go sit down. Wait. I'm turning on the oven. I've got the casserole in the oven.

Oh, good, Irene said. She finished her wine and poured another glass. She filled another glass with ice. I'll be with you in a minute. I'm going upstairs to check on the kids.

Florian lay on his stomach, with his pillow pressed over his head. Irene put her glass and the glass of ice on the bedside table and sat next to him. His bedspread was edged with geometric designs. The fabric in the middle was a landscape full of buffalo and eagles. She touched his shoulder and he turned over and took the pillow off. His eyes were his ancestor's eyes. There was a bruise rising on his forehead.

Irene tried to stroke his hair, but he jerked away.

I'm sorry. She sat there, and at last he let her touch him. This might seem strange, she said, but I've got my cell phone here. I'm going to take a picture of your face, honey, I'm sorry, but I have to.

Why?

Because it's important I can show somebody else.

Irene held her telephone up and took three pictures of Florian with his hand holding the hair off his face. His face was filled with tired sorrow.

Can you take this to a judge? It would be worth it if you could take it to a judge.

I'm going to try a counselor first, said Irene, I'm going to try and fix your dad.

You already tried to fix him, said Florian. Fuck him.

Stoney was at the door, with his lion, plus a bear, a moose, and an orange chicken.

Florian looked at Stoney and said, It's Charm Quark, the zookeeper. Don't worry. I'm okay, Stoney.

Why did you take his picture? asked Stoney.

Because I'm taking all your pictures, said Irene. She held up her cell phone. Stoney wandered off when his picture was done. He would put down his stuffed animals as soon as things were safe. He had baskets of different-size blocks he liked to build with. Cities and farms spread across his floor, with people and animals he made of clay, or he just used stones and pinecones that represented things that only Stoney knew.

Irene folded the ice in an old T-shirt and held the ice on Florian's forehead.

I think you'd better do the book report.

Florian's face went blank, then cold. He batted away the ice, balled his hands into fists, and pressed them on his temples.

Will you do the book report?

Florian nodded and whispered, Get out of here.

The dogs had followed her up the stairs and were quietly sitting outside the open door. One got up when she did. She gestured at Florian, and the other dog walked into Florian's room and put his head on the bed. The elegant plume of the dog's tail swept back and forth when Florian put his hand out. Irene went downstairs with the other dog at her heels. She could hear Gil talking on the telephone, laughing. She went into the kitchen and held her hands under the warm rushing tap of the sink. She wanted to stop her hands from shaking. At last she turned off the tap, dried her hands, and walked into the television room. She reached over, plucked the telephone from Gil's hands, and spoke into the receiver.

Say, can Gil call you back? We've got a little emergency.

Irene hit the End button and handed the phone back to Gil.

What the fuck?

Gil's face darkened with blood.

Irene turned the television off, then shut the door.

You need to get back into counseling.

Gil laughed. He gave the strange, rising, ho-ho-ho laugh, shaking his head, the laugh he used when he was being crossed and would retaliate. It was his better-watch-it laugh.

I've been there, Irene. Remember?

Yes, you went, but you quit after four months.

The shrink said I was okay. Remember? You were, and are, the one who needs help.

You hurt Florian.

Gil went silent. He looked away and put a knuckle to his mouth. When he looked back at Irene there were tears in his eyes.

You're right, he said. Oh god. Honey, I'm going up there to say I'm sorry. I really got carried away. I didn't mean to, as you know, I'd do anything in the world for Florian.

Gil stood up.

No, said Irene. She walked in front of the door. No, you can go later.

What, you're saying I can't apologize to my own son? Gil's voice vibrated on a softer level.

Listen to me, Gil. If you don't get into counseling I am going to leave you.

Gil opened and shut his mouth, then sat back down, abruptly. His face went dead white and a flush rose in his cheeks, hard red, as if he'd been slapped.

No, you said you wouldn't. You promised to stay with me. It was a promise.

Then you have to see a psychiatrist.

Okay. Gil grabbed a piece of paper and twisted it in his fingers, eyeing her. I guess I don't have any choice, he said at last, looking at Irene with hard eyes. That's hardly a prognosis for success. I'll go if we go together.

There's another way.

Gil shook his head.

You can let me go. Let me take the children.

No, said Gil. He began to shake his head rhythmically, back and forth. No, I'm sorry.

His eyes focused on her with sympathy.

No, you can't, he said. I don't like the way that looks. I'm sorry. If you try to leave me, then the children stay with me. We have been through this, you and I. We know the territory, Irene. I will take the children, and you know I can. I've kept track of your issues, Irene. Do you think a judge is going to give the children to a depressed, dysfunctional woman who drinks too much and can't support them? You can't work. You can't finish your degree. You're having trouble with this thing you're working on right now. You have how many pages? Six? I will have sole physical custody. They will be with me, Irene. He spoke emphatically, with a flat, chilling kindness. You know how I love them.

As Irene walked out of the room, she saw Riel frozen behind the stairs. While they were talking, Riel had slipped in the front door and taken her boots off. Gil had walked right past her when he went to open another wine bottle. Irene's eyes widened. Quickly, she turned and shut the door. She took Riel's hand and led her up the stairs. The muffled voices of the newscasters rose behind them.

How long were you hiding? How much did you hear?

Riel put her hand over her mouth.

The drastic part of Riel's plan was this: she would physically attack her father. The next time her father lashed out, Riel would too. She'd bite, kick, scratch like a wildcat. A cougar. A thing unafraid. She would be what she was—an Indian, only a *real* one. Stoic, with killer instincts. She'd make herself absorb all blows. She would damn the consequences. He'd have to respect above all else her craziness.

Gil knelt before Irene the next day and said, You are right. You are completely right. There's something wrong with me and I'm determined to address it. We'll go to a therapist, anything. I am going to spend more time with Florian, with the others. I am so, so, terribly sorry. But isn't it better to have an imperfect, spontaneous father? One who lets it all out, than it is to have a father who is screwed up and can't express himself? Or no father at all? No father at all would be the worst, as we know, Irene. Better to have an occasional asshole like me, Irene, than the absence of a father. Don't give up on me, love. I can make myself into the one you want, love. I can be the father that our children deserve. I have failed you all, each one of you, in unique and separate ways, and I will make it up to you, each one of you, in ways that will convince you each how much I love you. Because I do love you, Irene, and I do love the children. With every bone in my body and atom in my heart, I love you. Here, he said, look, and he opened catalogs of musical instruments. We should each have a musical instrument, he said, perhaps this acoustic guitar for you, look, it's the color of cinnamon, and an electric guitar for Florian, a piano would be surprising, lessons, or a silver flute. Can't you see Stoney playing a silver flute? He'd look like a little piper boy, a Greek demigod, a forest creature. And Riel, that's difficult, but Riel I think would play some sort of woodwind, or with her sense of humor an accordion. He flipped through a catalog and pointed out the pearlized box of an accordion with lovely black keys.

In her new efforts at observation, Riel noticed many things. For instance, she had noticed that the dogs were behaving as if their humans were going on a trip. The dogs hated it whenever the suitcases came out. But there were no suitcases. They only acted as if there were suitcases. They were nervously watchful these days. There was something in the air that made them uneasy. With her newly honed senses Riel could feel it too. It was something specific that she didn't want to name, though ordinarily she could name anything.

One of her notebooks was filled now with memories of the past. The other notebook was possible scenarios of the future. She could name any number of frightful scenarios because she had made a list of them, and how an Indian would survive. The first thing about being prepared is to take the future seriously. As she thought about these things, Riel became more and more certain how her family would behave.

First and foremost, she was certain that, when disaster struck, she would be the one left behind.

If there was a sudden panic, a bomb launched toward Minneapolis, an asteroid targeted to hit the Walker Center, a 100 percent fatal pandemic virus, an airplane exploding the

IDS Tower, a vampire uprising, if Indian killers or born-again Nazis or nuclear winter took over the U.S. government, if any of these things happened and the family had to flee, she would be left behind.

She would be left behind because she was the quiet one. Even quieter now! She blended into her surroundings. Took on the shapes of things. Made sure she didn't matter or stand out at family dinner or when they all watched TV together. Of course, she cataloged everything and observed with clear eyes. And though quiet, she was not a mouse, or if so, she was a brave mouse. She never crept or hid. She walked upright, barefooted, silent with an Indian art. She knew every creak in the elegant old house. She could dart soundlessly anywhere. She'd taken a can of WD-40 and oiled the hinges on the doors that the children used, but left the squeak in her father's studio and her parents' bathroom and bedroom. Yet when her father got angry, she did not always take advantage of her knowledge and vanish. She tried to make herself breathe. She tried to make herself think. Sometimes she chose, like the dogs, to walk toward his anger.

She had acquitted herself, according to her compilations of memory, courageously half the time. Cowardly the other half. She was working toward her surprise attack by reading the book she had sneaked from her mother's office. She was still reading the Catlin letters, the part about the bloody training of Mandan warriors especially, over and over. She hadn't got the courage yet to pierce her skin, but she was hardening herself to blows. At night, she struck herself with a ruler. She slapped her own face. She stood in painful positions, held her breath underwater in the bathtub, pulled her hair, and raised bruises on her legs. She would be prepared.

Yet she would be left behind, she was sure.

Stoney would be afraid, so her mother would take him first. Florian would be marched to the car, her father yelling at him not to slouch. The two they noticed. And it would be tragic when they drove off without her—tragic for them. Several reasons. As she couldn't train horses, like the Mandan, she held the hearts of the dogs, and they would stay with her, of course. Also, she was the only one in the family who was developing her survival skills. Without her, they would perish.

Riel had put together an emergency tote bag and stashed it underneath her bed. It was an old pink Workout Barbie bag with a water-bottle net on the side. Riel kept the bottle filled. Inside the bag, she had matches dipped in wax, a Baggie full of them. She had a flashlight, extra batteries, a cigarette lighter left behind at a party, two permanent markers, and a pad of paper. She had read about pemmican, and decided the best substitute would be granola bars. She'd stashed between six and twelve granola bars (sometimes she ate one at night and forgot to replace it for a few days). She had dry dog food. Duct tape. Krazy Glue. Money. Indians would not have needed Krazy Glue or money but, she reasoned, she was a contemporary Indian. A mixture of old and new. She had also taken from her mother's old camping gear a bottle of water purification tablets and a space blanket. Her plan when left behind (if it was summer) was to take a boogie board from the back hall closet, strap her Barbie bag on it, then swim out to the middle of the lake with her dogs, and set up camp on one of the islands. She and the dogs would stay there, just as she'd told her mother, living on fish and granola bars, until the emergency was over.

So yes, she was the one with survival skills. She read up on how to bait a hook and had caught fish before. She now knew how to start a fire even in the rain and how to construct a shelter out of brush. She had taken to watching *Survivorman*— the closest to an old-time Indian on TV. She would eat bugs and recently dead squirrels, or whatever. She had watched the geese around the lake and was pretty sure she could catch one. She even knew what plants though bitter were edible. Her family, meanwhile, had forgotten their heritage. Yes, they would regret not having her along. And she would regret their horror when they were locked in a giant Rubik's of jammed traffic trying to leave the city.

Suddenly, one of them says her name. Her mother screams, tries to jump from the car and go back after her. Her father says, No, you'll die too. Better we are alive to protect the children we have left to us. Stoney begins to cry. But Florian stares out of the window and smiles, knowing Riel is better off. Remembering she has the dogs. He says nothing. It is going to be a long, long drive, probably to no-where. His thoughts will keep him sane even as the rest of them revert to animals. Florian will come staggering back in a few years with a sickening story that includes treachery, an accident, cannibalism. Guilt on the part of Riel's mother for eating her husband and secretly feeding parts of his body to her children. She may be too ashamed to come out of hiding. Florian and Riel and the dogs will guard the house and repel intruders until their mother overcomes her shame and returns.

Will she bring Stoney back with her? That is a matter that requires some thought. If Stoney has stopped speaking, it may be because he recognized the ring on the hand he was eating as his father's wedding band. But surely, no, their mother would of course have disguised the meat in a stew with stolen vegeta-bles. Although their mother cannot tell them, she was always, secretly, on their side.

If she didn't play things so fucking close to her chest, I would not have started this, thought Gil, entering Irene's office. Un-healthy compulsion, and now the shrink. He'd agreed. Under duress! But he did not dread seeing the therapist; in fact, it gave him hope. Of course the therapist would see things his way, and with the therapist on his side, fighting for his family, Irene would slowly be persuaded that he was worth another try. A real try. No lover in the wings.

He hadn't lost his temper in a long time, but when he apologized, Florian not only had forgiven him but had told him that Irene had taken a picture of the bruise on his forehead. He'd hugged Florian and told him what a magnificent son he was over and over; now they were very close again. And Irene, well, he'd gotten up early every morning and made elaborate breakfasts for the children—French toast stuffed with crème fraîche, omelets, fruit shakes—plus she was still considering the musical instruments. He could take the issue of the photograph up with her some other time. Or just erase it from her phone.

He opened her diary and caught up with the trivia of their days, which he enjoyed, but he had to read the words *I am faithful to Gil for the obvious reasons* three times before it penetrated. She has not broken trust. She is mine.

It was like the ground stopped shaking.

He sat stunned in the chair. After a while, he realized that tears were running down his face, dripping onto his collar. He laughed and wiped his cheeks with the heel of his palm. Tears were still coming. He laughed some more and shook his head. He had closed himself off, become suspicious, spied on her. She had no idea—he double-checked every credit card charge and phone bill. Sometimes, even

with the children in the car, he managed to drive around
the lake just to make sure she was really taking a walk.

There's Mommy! one of them would point and call
out.

Let's turn off here, he'd answer, and let her have her privacy!

He'd persuaded their friends to question her, discreetly,
dropping hints about their own infidelities. And all this time,
she had been faithful, for the obvious reasons. He sat back,
held his fingers to his lips.

The obvious reasons. What were they?

That night he took a walk with Irene. He tried to hold her
hand, but she shook him off. She had the dogs strapped to
her waist with a belt leash. She wore slick-soled shoes. The
dogs lunged forward, pulling her through the icy residen-
tial streets. They picked up speed and loped like wolves.
Irene wore a slim black coat. Her arms were raised like a
dancer's. She glided eerily in and out of the chiaroscuro
of street lamps. Gil caught his breath as he watched her
fly strangely through the night. His thought was that she
would disappear. Something would happen. She would be

drawn faster and faster into the dark and he would never see her again.

Then one dog got excited and jumped over the other. The leads tangled and all three went down in the snow. Gil ran forward to help her up, but his alarm lingered. What he'd seen looked like stage wizardry or something out of a dream. She had such physical confidence. She did crazy things like this. She'd flown so fast. He hoped she wouldn't try it again.

I should go to Washington, said Irene, laughing as she rose and dusted herself off. She arranged the dogs in front of her again and they started off, walking together now.

Washington. In spite of the diary, Gil's thoughts lurched suspiciously toward Germaine, whose job took him there often. Irene hated to travel. He took her hand. She drew it out of his grip.

I should go and see some Catlins, she explained.

Jealousy flicked up in Gil like a struck match. I don't get how you can keep looking at his images. They're all alike. Why should you go? He tried to douse his little flame by challenging Irene.

I don't think he was a great painter, she said. Not like you.

She said it nastily, still punishing him.

Do you think I am, he said, his voice forlorn. Catlin happened to hit the moment, Irene. One year his subjects were alive, the next year they were dead. The moment can happen to any artist and his art becomes important regardless of his skill. Maybe I'm just bullshit, Irene, maybe it's all nothing. How do you know if you're really good at what you do or you've just hit a moment? Gil's voice shook with sympathy for himself. After a while he answered his questions, his voice tentative. I haven't hit a moment, I don't think. In fact, the times are against me. Indians have fallen out of fashion again.

Even for a narcissist that's quite a statement, said Irene.

You should paint white people. She grabbed his hand, swung it like a girl, and picked up their pace. The demographics are shifting! They're the vanishing people. You should document their ride into the sunset.

Gil decided to feel forgiven instead of insulted. She kept his hand as they walked in and out of a streetlight. As they walked on and on after that and she did not drop his hand, his heart lifted. His disquiet and even the hurt feelings fell away, and he was suddenly buoyant. It struck him that he could be hopeful, why not? She hadn't fallen for Germaine's dark skin and enrollment number. Or his intelligence or kindness, either. An ice fog hung in the air and Gil became entranced with the way it shifted and distorted the lights that streamed out all around them, bouncing off the neatly snowbound streets and black windows and the slick iron fences and the torn tips of the trees.

I'm going to see Florian's teacher tomorrow, said Irene. His English teacher.

That idiot! said Gil, happy. Some teacher. He wouldn't know a good paper if it smacked him between the eyes. I don't care what he says. Florian's an A student. The guy's a jealous twit!

Irene settled into one of the student desks in the classroom and took off her scarf.

Is everything all right at home? asked Mr. Graham. The students called the English teacher Graham Cracker, or just Cracker. Florian only called him Cracker and Irene thought of him as Cracker, too. A young man, but dry and brittle.

I guess, said Irene. I guess so. Why? I mean, I'm here to talk about Florian's paper. Why?

Florian seems rather, what's the word—cut off, isolated?

Isolated? Florian's back and forth because of his math classes at the U. So I guess, said Irene, it's just a little hard to make friends.

Let me be frank. May I be frank?

Irene spoke over him. And *Lord of the Flies*. That's such a grim book and Florian's outlook is already pretty bleak, which is why I am wondering whether Florian could make up for that report with extra reading. Only not *A Separate*

Peace or *Catcher in the Rye* or anything that ends with a, you know . . . Because to tell you the truth, things are not so good at home.

Then I *will* be frank and tell you that your visit is fortuitous because Florian came in with a bruise on his forehead and I asked him about that and he mentioned his father. Now I'm obliged as an educator to report that. I think the world of Florian. We think Florian has a very sensitive and unique outlook that needs nurturing.

We?

Florian's other teachers as well as myself. You and I have talked about this before. I know we have. It should come as no surprise to you. Florian has the capability to do extraordinary work someday and at this point he should be visiting some top-notch colleges and he should be sitting in on classes, say, at MIT and you should be making certain that his life is as supportive and sustaining as possible, as his mother. You, of course, are the one responsible for giving him the stability that he needs in order to flourish.

Yes, said Irene.

An uncomfortable silence. Cracker, thin and intense, shifted back and forth in his desk chair.

I suppose it's not easy living in a house with two geniuses.

Florian is a genius, said Irene. My husband is a very good painter.

Cracker looked down at his papers. Since we have talked,

he said, there is no need for me to report, no need for this to go any further, not as long as I know that from now on you are going to protect your son.

I am going to do that, said Irene. She lay her scarf on the desk between them. But if it comes to—and I'm exploring this but please, keep this confidential—if I have to leave Gil and it comes to support for my obtaining custody, I have to ask if you will testify that you did notice the bruise.

I would, I would, but if I did, there would be the question why didn't I report it at the time? So you see, you've got to do something. I can only be so much help.

I see. Well you've been, I won't exactly say helpful. But your heart's in the right place where Florian is concerned.

Yes, it is. You can count on that.

Then will you please assign him something cheerful?

Young people, said Cracker, do not like cheerful stories. They like tragic and brutal ones. You know that.

I suppose you're right, said Irene. I suppose they want to be reassured. She spoke almost to herself. They want to look at the tragedy and brutality from the outside, from a safe distance, don't they? Don't they want to know that these things—wars, killings, being orphaned, abandoned—these things will not happen to them? They will not be left alone to fend for themselves? They will not be hurt?

Everyone gets hurt, said Cracker.

It shouldn't happen, said Irene.

I'll do everything I can for him, but I can't do your job. Cracker reached out to give Irene's scarf back, but she yanked it from his fingertips.

The sun came out, as it always did after Gil lost his temper. For days, things were peaceful and easy. Florian got a C on his book report, but did the extra work after Irene talked to Cracker and managed to raise the grade to an A-. Irene took the children to the winter powwow, where they sat with Louise and Bobbi, who was very beautiful, a Mohawk woman with blond hair and cruel, sexy, perfectly sculpted thin lips. The drum was too loud to really talk, so they either yelled at each other or waited for a pause between songs. Bobbi said to Irene that she'd make dance outfits for her children.

You would?

In spite of her cruel lips, Bobbi had an easygoing way. She seemed utterly sincere.

Irene gazed at Bobbi in amazement. That's a lot of work, she said, too much work.

She's not kidding, said Louise. She'll really do it.

Bobbi's youngest son was out on the floor. His grass dance outfit was black and red with narrow white ribbons that flowed and shifted with his steps. There was complex embroidery and beadwork across the shirt. He wore bobbing plumes and moved confidently, a little man, rippling like imaginary grass.

Florian said, Damn, he's good!

Remember this, the announcer cried out when the drum stopped, this is your land, this is all Indian land!

Riel took Irene's hand excitedly and hugged her. Mom, you hear that? This is all Indian land!

Gidebwe, said Irene.

You have to teach me to talk Indian, said Riel.

Sure.

Not sure. Indian sure.

Geget igo! laughed Irene. She remembered almost none of the Ojibwe she'd been taught.

Riel was elated. She repeated the phrases under her breath. Her face was fiercely alert as the dancers whirled and leapt.

You're the one, said Bobbi, making a kissing motion at Riel. I'm gonna make yours first. What's your style?

Riel watched the dancers flash by, the swirling shawls, the sonar clatter of bone breastplates and jingles. The jingle dancers lifted their fans at the four loudest beats and Riel breathed out, *Those ones.*

Afterward, the children were wild in Irene's car, like other people's children, happy, mouthy, full of the sound of the drum and cotton candy.

Let's just keep driving, said Riel, when they got near the house.

So they drove around and around the lake in deep cold. The snow had frozen, suspended and sparkling in the air. The sky was deep blue when they finally piled through the door. Gil said that he was working a painting to the finish and could not leave his studio. Actually, he was making calls. Putting finishing touches on plans for the party. Now that he knew Irene was his, that she was faithful, he wanted more than ever to give her a perfect, memorable night. Still, he did not call Louise up and cancel his request for her to stay with Irene that day. He still wanted to know—what was wrong with knowing? He wanted to know what she did without him.

Germaine? This is Gil.

Gil.

I know, I know. It's been a while. Say, I just wanted to invite you to Irene's birthday party. November 30th. On the off chance, you know, that you and Lissa are in town next week, why don't you come over to the house? It's a surprise party.

We're not in town.

Oh, really? I thought you were visiting here fairly often.

No.

Still, just on the off chance, the invitation is open.

We won't be there.

Is Portland working out for you?

There was a stiff silence. Gil rolled his eyes.

I'll let you go. Just a thought.

Gil hung up the phone. Then picked it up again and smashed it down on the receiver.

Some fucking friend you were, he said. But you didn't manage, did you. You didn't quite manage! Back to your foundation boards, asshole.

Florian shambled into the kitchen, opened the cupboard, the refrigerator, and poured himself a glass of milk.

How were things today? said Gil. He pushed his hair back, retied the small club ponytail at the base of his neck. Did things go well?

In a general sense?

Florian drank off the first glass of milk and poured another.

Don't drink all of the milk now, Florian. Leave some for the rest of us.

Mom got two gallons.

Gil looked at Florian, irritated, but then he was taken by surprise by his son's beauty. Florian wasn't wearing his glasses and his narrow brown eyes, picked out by short, perfect spikes of straight lashes, burned darkly against his pale skin. His hair came to a peak at the center of his hairline and shot forward in a tuft. The way Florian slumped his hips against the counter as he drank was unknowing, pre-sexual. He was going to be very handsome. As Florian was leaving the room, Gil called out, I love you.

He heard Florian's footsteps pause.

At that moment, Florian was passing the rippling antique mirror that hung over the sideboard in the dining room. When he was younger, he'd avoided looking in the mirror because it dimmed and distorted images. It was almost like seeing people moving underwater. His father had followed him and paused now in the doorway behind Florian. In the mirror, their eyes met, and it seemed to Florian at that moment they were both underwater and he gasped for breath, painfully, his heart pinching.

I love you, too, Dad, he said.

Gil touched his son's shoulder as he passed him. He'd thought of painting Florian drinking the milk, standing against the counter, one hand on the wood, the black T-shirt, the jeans, bare feet. A boy drinking milk. Through that act both separated and linked to his mother. Gil thought of Irene and the portrait he was working on and he went upstairs, thinking that if he could possibly finish it before Irene's birthday he could give it to her. She did not have an *America*. They'd always had to sell them immediately. He kept working on the dead-looking portrait and was also finishing an old one he'd started a year before.

In that picture, Irene had turned away; she was hunched over something, hiding it. She was glancing at someone just out of the frame. Her hand was between her legs. She was doglike, he thought, guarding her little bone, her sex. As if he wanted to steal it! That little moment with Florian was forgotten. Just hearing Germaine's voice had pushed his buttons. But, Gil reminded himself, his thoughts suddenly clearing, she is faithful. He smiled and opened the french doors that led out onto a small balcony. He stepped into the icy wind. Immediately, as freezing air sliced through his shirt, he was seized by a rough tumult of elation.

Irene walked through the lobby of the hotel. The floor was made of a rosy stone veined with peach and rust. A clean, bitter wood trimmed the hallways and doors. There was an arrangement of twisted willow and bronze-petaled flowers with acid green tongues. Facing the shiny metal door as she waited for the elevator, she saw distress and need form on her face. This was the same hotel where, for a matter of hours, she had been happy with Germaine. They'd hardly spoken. The sheets were heavy and she had been aware of their bodies vaguely moving in a curved golden mirror. Irene stepped into the elevator, hit the button, and closed her eyes. She got out on the third floor and walked into the restaurant, where she was meeting Louise. Just as she remembered, the napkins were starched, folded into fans. At their lunch, Germaine had carefully unfolded the napkin and she had watched his hands smooth the stiff cloth. He wasn't thinking about what he was doing, but his hands had an alertness all of their own. He'd run his fingers along the tablecloth and cupped the glass in his palm. Many times since, Irene had thought of the things his hands had done in the hour before he had touched her.

When Irene reached the table, Louise got up and hugged her, messily, still cheerfully chewing. She was eating the bread off Irene's bread plate.

Sorry, you were late.

Irene put her cell phone on the table. She would answer it if the number of the children's school came up. She took such a deep breath that she felt light-headed.

I'm going to tell her, she thought. I'm going to tell her that I am leaving Gil. If I tell just one person, I can do it. She will be the person.

Louise, she said.

Wait! More bread, please?

Louise made an elaborate show of getting more bread. Now that Irene was here, she was uncomfortable, embarrassed. It had not upset her when Gil had called her up and asked for her help in creating a party for Irene. She was complimented, touched, to be included in the event. Gil's request that she question and follow Irene after their lunch had surprised her, though, and at first she'd been unable to answer. Then she quickly realized that if she did not help Gil out with this part of the planning, someone else would follow Irene all day. And who knows why Gil wanted that? So she had agreed.

You're quiet, said Irene. Are you okay?

Just hungry.

Should she spoil the surprise for Irene by telling her that, when she returned home, Gil and their friends would be waiting with champagne and cake and gifts? Beautifully wrapped gifts? Like the one in the trunk of her car?

So how's your son? We never talked about him. Irene ordered hot tea.

He's doing fine. His dad's got him this week. Do you know Ray DeChardin? Teaches engineering at the U? He's married, two little ones. My boy likes going over there; he has his own room. The wife's, you know, okay. She's Navajo, or Dine, really quiet and small and pretty.

I remember Ray's braids. Down to his waist.

His braids are skinny now. They used to be fat. The fat went to his stomach. But he's a good guy. He was always more thoughtful, stable, than he looked.

Louise asked what Irene's thesis was about. Irene started talking about Catlin and how he had wounded a buffalo and then sketched and painted it as it slowly died. He described the process in one of his letters. He goaded the buffalo into a fury every time it tried to lie down and die. It had broken a leg, so it couldn't charge him.

He could be cruel to get the picture, she said, but he loved Indians. We broke him, broke his health, broke his heart. Stole the greatest comforts of his life. All because he found our world irresistible.

Irene knew that she'd kept talking because she was afraid to say that she was leaving Gil.

Louise put her hand on Irene's hand where it rested on the table.

Hey, said Louise, I've got to ask you something.

Wait, said Irene, I've got to tell you something.

Is it about a surprise?

In a way, said Irene.

Louise's hand still rested on top of her hand, as if Louise had forgotten where she put it. Irene turned her hand over and their palms touched. Louise's was warm and dry. She was sensible, substantial.

Irene grabbed her hand. I'm so glad you're going to be my sister. Mine, right? Irene's pulse beat in her throat. If I tell you this, you won't tell Gil?

Louise drew her hand back into her lap. She was sure that Irene was going to ask her to keep some secret regarding an affair. Why else would Gil have asked Louise to follow her? She hadn't counted on lying to Gil. She was a bad liar.

Maybe you shouldn't tell me, said Louise.

They stared at each other; Irene's face went hot and she couldn't swallow.

They didn't know each other well enough yet to unstick the text from the subtext. They began to eat, spiking their food up warily. They began to talk about their children—a neutral and absorbent topic.

Gil had everyone park their cars down the street, away from the side of the house with the driveway where Irene would enter with the children after she picked them up. He'd taken the dogs to a kennel so they would not disrupt the guests. He'd set his gifts in their bedroom—white roses, white nightgown, white Japanese robe, a perfume called White Nocturne.

Louise had parked well away from the house, and carried her gift in her arms up the sanded sidewalk. She held it too carefully, walked reluctantly. The gift was fragile, but not breakable. A gauzy gray scarf. Inside, she gave it to Gil, who asked her where she'd met Irene. At this question, Louise felt a sudden jolt of guilty rage.

As you know, I asked her to lunch, she said.

Where else did she go?

What's wrong with you? Louise pushed her face up into his face. People milled past them. What the fuck is wrong with you?

Oh, said Gil, charmingly, do I seem the jealous husband? I guess I do. Can you blame me? Here she comes, look!

Louise turned away and decided to walk straight out the back door, not pausing, but Gil swept her with the others, into a large room off the hall. The dining room. It was filled with food and lighted by dozens of white wax tapers.

Car doors slammed out in the driveway. A moment later the outside door opened and the children approached, talking. Irene walked into the room.

Surprise! Louise yelled with everyone else.

Irene looked straight at her and was flooded with the realization that Louise had collaborated secretly with Gil. Gil was right beside Louise now, thanking her. Does surprise look the same as betrayal, Irene wondered, widening her eyes. She was sick with disappointment. *The two of them, after all.* Maybe now I will never get out.

Happy birthday, darling! Gil cried.

Then everything erupted in noise. Gil took the children in his arms. Louise vanished. The party began to swirl.

Standing in the golden shadows with a glass of champagne in her fingers, Irene thought she'd better blur away, and put the glass to her lips.

They made love that night with a grappling violence, as if secret selves stepped out of their skins. She left her nails long and ragged. He covered her mouth and pinned back her head. They had extinguished all the candles and lamps and even the porch lights. Everything in the house was dead black, and hollow with the afterparty emptiness of littered rooms. The children had gone away with the families of friends. There was the eerie absence of the dogs. The two went on and on in utter blackness, unable to either come to a climax or stop. He made her say all of the things he wanted to hear. She gave him the belt to the white kimono and he tied it around her throat.

When she woke up, naked and aching, she was still tied to the bed.

When the children came home the next morning, there was still the strange hush. They went into their rooms and played or did their homework all day, quietly, as if they sensed their parents' exhaustion. Their faces were remote and watchful as Irene fed them lunch, then dinner. When they crept toward Irene to say good night, their hot whispers were hoarse and fearful. She held them and told them it was going to be all right. *What? What is going to be all right?* They clutched her arms, insistent, until Gil told them to get moving.

The story of The Mink, which Irene had falsified, was part of another story, much longer and more complex. In the same year, 1832, Catlin had painted a Dakota chief who possessed considerable force of character. Little Bear was painted in profile, which gave his rival, the dishonorable Sunka, or The Dog, an excuse for hurling at Little Bear a grave insult. The other half of Little Bear, said Sunka, was no good, worthless, shameful. He was but half a man. Their fury turned deadly and Little Bear was hit by a gun blast to that very side of his face that Catlin had not depicted. Little Bear died of his dreadful wound, and The Dog was hunted down and slain by warriors faithful to Little Bear.

The strangeness of the story lies in the *profil perdu*, the lost profile, which both inspired and predicted the actual loss of the man and was for Catlin but an instinctive aesthetic choice based on whim, an artist's fancy, or boredom perhaps at having made so many similar full-face portraits.

Catlin's painting aroused suspicion, caused death. The tribes Catlin visited were artistic and produced extraordinary objects, including pictorial art. Mahtotohpa, Four Bears, presented George Catlin a buffalo robe upon which the chief had painted the deadly exploits that composed his life story. The paintings were complex, symbolic, dramatic, exquisite. They were also one-dimensional and contained no shadows. In addition to so many other European inventions—steel knives, iron kettles, guns, hatchets, trade beads, leg-hold traps, and a newspaper that was purchased by an Indian at great cost and used as medicine—Catlin brought shadows.

Because of the shadows, his paintings had the direct force and power of the supernatural, the dream replica, the doppelgänger. It was as if a sudden twin had been created right before the subject. A twin that seemed to live and breathe and follow one with its eyes and yet was motionless. The paintings were objects of veneration and of fear. Some swore uneasily that those who allowed their portraits to be painted, eyes open, would not lie peacefully after death, as some aspect of their beings would live on, staring out at the world. Others, disturbed that Catlin painted buffalo and took them away with him in his portfolio, tied his actions to the increasing scarcity of the herds upon which their lives depended. So it was, the shadows actually stole their subjects and, for the rest of the world, became more real, until it seemed they were the only things left.

There were times that Irene and Gil grew so exhausted with the struggle that they simply walked out of their trenches and embraced over the heads of their children. King's X was declared. The whole family was in love. Just after the party, a great snow fell and the family had one such wonderful night. Snow-laden branches crashed onto the power lines somewhere, cutting off electricity to houses in that area of the city. Riel and Stoney had been watching television in the basement and groped their way upstairs. Florian's computer screen went off and he came down calling to his parents. Gil was walking out of the kitchen. Irene was walking in. They collided softly and held each other for a moment. The silent dogs balanced their attention among them all, herding them into one room.

Where are the candles?

I know, they're in the junk drawer!

And matches?

Matches are with them.

A snick of a match. The flare of light upon their mother's smiling and excited face. She loved small disasters.

What should we do? What should we do? cried Stoney.

Let's each take a candle and go outside, Irene said.

She stuck five candles through small paper plates so the wax would not drip on their hands. They put on coats and boots, took up their candles, and went outdoors with the dogs. Outside, Irene lighted their candles and the radiance flew up their faces. Snow had fallen earlier that afternoon, and Gil theorized that it had grown too heavy somewhere and knocked out a transformer. Irene laughed and said, Do you even know what a transformer does? And Gil, instead of taking offense, laughed with her and cried: Transforms! Transforms everything! They walked along in candlelight, admiring the quiet houses with snowdrift trim. Lights moved mysteriously, deep in hidden rooms behind dark windows, but no one else was outdoors.

The snow gave off its own radiance, and the low clouds reflected the street lamps, still alight but on a lower emergency power. The sky was a startling orange. They walked all the way to the park's ball field. The field was swept down to an inch of hard and perfect snow. Their candles had burned so low that it was dangerous for the children to keep them in their hands, so they stuck them around the sides of home base. The park light cast blurred shadows on the snow. Irene said that this would be the perfect place to play shadow tag, a game she had played as a child, under summer street lamps. So they began playing tag by touching shadows. Irene and Gil ran and whirled, stepping in and out of each other's darkness. The children dipped and slid, leapt away so that their shadows unfurled beneath them. The dogs galloped in circles around the family to keep them from straying. Gil found a place just under the light where he could hide his shadow tightly under his feet. Irene and the children arranged themselves around him, laughing. As they were closing in to capture Gil, he leapt out. His shadow sprang across the field.

Part II

T welve years before his death, F. Scott Fitzgerald wrote a story that contains these beautiful sentences: *It isn't given to us to know those rare moments when people are wide open and the lightest touch can wither or heal. A moment too late and we can never reach them any more in this world. They will not be cured by our most efficacious drugs or slain with our sharpest swords.*

The last words of the quotation were troubling to Gil, but he thought of the first part often in relation to Irene. This unknowable moment the writer spoke of had a powerful effect on his actions, for he did believe that there were interstices, cracks, apertures, gaps, in the wall between them. That wall was made of an immaterial rubble. Things said and unsaid, actions, misunderstandings, a piled conglomerate of moments, which, he believed, one *pure* moment could pierce. Or one symbol. Or one metaphor. What he really thought was that there would come a moment where he could truly reach Irene and that moment would change everything.

Irene herself had told him to resist the lure of moments, but that was the problem of history, teasing out the right moments. It was a problem in painting, too—the right moment. Sometimes one brushstroke could change the moment, but that was what Gil loved: that very fine edge between moments when the painting came into existence. Irene said he was addicted to the idea of pivotal moments in life and in art because he'd watched so much TV, but he quoted Fitzgerald and also argued that every great painting was about a moment.

Yes, she said, *lots* of them. They build. The greatest paintings are never just *one* moment. Look at Rembrandt's late self-portraits, she said, every moment he ever lived is in his eyes and on his face.

Oh, please, said Gil. *Hendrickje Bathing*. A delicious moment. And Bonnard's self-portrait in the bathroom mirror? Humble, spent. His life was gone by then. But you can see it—he is not pathetic—unshakable lucidity in that moment.

All moments— said Irene, but Gil raised his voice.

Bonnard's self-portrait is exactly about the moment! You have never understood time in the context of a painting!

This was another of their enjoyable arguments. Once they made an issue neutral, they could talk for hours. One thing: they were never bored with each other. They might hate each other, at least, Irene might hate Gil, while he had no idea how much he hated Irene because he was so focused on winning back her love. He really did hate her. That was part of his immaterial wall. He couldn't see it or experience this hatred, but it was there. Part of his fantasy about the breach in the wall had to do with reaching through his own hatred, which he didn't know existed.

So.

Gil had a wall. Irene had a wall. Between the two walls there was a neutral, untouched area, a wilderness of all they did not know and could not imagine about the other person. Gil actually had a clear picture of this space between them. He saw it as an untouched Eden like the Korean Demilitarized Zone.

9 A.M. December 4. On their first visit to a marriage counselor, a pleasant and maternal woman of sixty-two, no fool, but full of heart, Gil described this imaginary landscape. He spoke in a soft, sincere voice.

I see Irene and myself on opposite sides of the DMZ, cut off by razor wire, sharp defenses, intelligence, if you will. Between us there is a strip of longing and love that belongs to both of us, untouched.

Yes, said the therapist, I know about the real DMZ.

It harbors incredible biodiversity. It is extraordinarily beautiful, said Gil.

Your point? asked the therapist.

The red-capped crane is there, symbol of peace, said Gil.

I don't think the red-capped crane is the symbol of peace, said Irene.

Again, your point? asked the therapist.

I think we can get there, to the DMZ. Gil hushed, hung his head.

After a moment the therapist addressed Irene.

What do you think, Irene?

The metaphor was tempting. She'd heard that this two-mile swath, protected by walls and chain link and continually patrolled, was filled with life extinct elsewhere, and that made it sacred. She wanted to go there herself, this place untouched since before she was even born.

She sighed and looked at Gil, at the therapist, and asked, What if one of us develops nuclear weapons?

Gil and the therapist became reflective, and there was the hissing sound of forced air flowing through the vents.

You already have them, said Gil suddenly. He leaned toward her, intent. The question is, Will you use them?

So I'm North Korea?

Yes, said Gil gently, I think you are.

Wait, said the therapist.

So I'm freaking Kim Jong Il with the weird haircut and those crazy totalitarian mass games?

I'm afraid so, said Gil.

No way, said Irene, I want to be South Korea with the female executives and the animation experts. I want to be an Asian tiger.

Wait, said the therapist.

Because I think you are North Korea, said Irene. You have

taken our children hostage and trained your big old warhead on me.

My warhead?

Stop, the therapist commanded.

Yes, your warhead, and it's not so big. It's dinky, dinky, dinky.

No, said Gil, it is not. I'm well above the national average. Do you know the national average for penile length? He addressed the therapist.

I don't know if I can help you two, she said. You're dithering around. You're not addressing any pertinent issues. You're playing games. Are you serious about this work?

Of course, said Gil. I apologize. I am serious.

He gets lost in his own metaphors, said Irene. They pile up while he forgets the picture. He can't see what he's painting anymore.

Who. Whom I'm painting.

Me.

There was silence.

Irene, can you say more about that? The therapist waited.

Gil frowned at his hands, flexed his fingers.

Well, if she's not going to say anything, I—

Wait, said the therapist.

Gil looked down at his hands again, folded his fingers tightly in his lap.

Paper cranes, Gil said, musingly, the bird of peace.

The dove, Irene hissed.

The therapist looked stern. Let's let Irene finish her thought.

Okay, said Irene, you can have your cranes. Just stop driving Florian crazy, stop hitting the children, stop scaring us. They aren't your children anyway. I had all three of them with other men. Separate men.

Please, said Gil. He was looking at Irene. Please, is it true?

Just kidding, said Irene.

December 4, 2007

RED DIARY

Florian has skin much like Gil's, heavy Irish skin that won't take a tan but stubbornly burns. His brown hair has a hint of my mother's red. His eyes, though. His eyes are so dark you cannot tell the pupil from the iris. His eyes are gifts from our ancestors, I always say, but the truth is different.

Florian's father was an academic, a world-renowned historian—kind of a genius, like Florian. I met him at a conference. We went back up to his room after a lecture, and I discovered that although he was pale and thin his prick was huge and merciless.

Irene threw down the pen, laughing. Huge and merciless! Besides, when did I ever go to a conference? Or meet anyone world-renowned? If he's jealous enough to fall for that, Gil deserves to suffer. She went on writing, filling up weeks of pages.

Huge and merciless. You would never have guessed. We ordered room service for two days—he missed the panel discussions and all of the other panelists knew why. People started to address his empty chair. Somebody set a room key on it. It was a nice hotel and I stole a pair of silver butter tongs, a souvenir. Florian's father's silver butter tongs. All I have!

Ridiculous.

I nearly blurted out the truth in our first therapy session. Luckily, it was too incredible—I am sure Gil thought I was just making a cruel joke.

Riel's brown hair is exactly my color. Her skin is changeable, from delicate cream to rich bronze. In winter, she is pale as a white peach so that the blush of her cheeks is a fairy-tale contrast. As soon as the sun strikes her in summer, her skin blooms an even gold. It is as though the sun actually comes up inside of her.

She glows. I see it happen every year. Again, a gift, but from a man Gil knows very well and considers a friend—I wonder if Gil will ever guess that when he was in New York at an opening we made love in Gil's studio. Right upstairs. Then downstairs, in our bed, our marital bed. I still feel somewhat guilty that we both made fun of Gil—it wasn't right of us, I know.

Irene stopped again, thinking: As if Gil would believe me writing "marital bed"! He'll be clued in—this is all so trashy—he'll know I'm writing it to hurt him. Then she began to write again, more thoughtfully.

Stoney has skin a shade deeper than either Gil or I and his eyes are green. A true, translucent green. Nobody we can think of on either side of the family has ever had these green eyes before, but we credit some beautiful Metis in the near past, never photographed. Because he was born after we'd begun to have our troubles, Gil may suspect, though he's never said as much, that he is not Stoney's father. It is true that we made our baby in Paris, as I have told him. He was not made the week after or the week before. However, he has nothing to do with Gil. Not one molecule. He was given to me by Our Lady of Notre Dame. His green eyes will take him back to Paris someday, where he will walk the streets in a familiar dream and perhaps meet others, an old man with green eyes. His father.

None of the children have one molecule in common with Gil.

What you said today was so terrible, so hurtful; we need to talk about it, Gil said to Irene that afternoon.

I know, said Irene, I'm sorry. What a sick thing to say.

Our children are mine, then, said Gil.

Oh, Gil, said Irene. How could I have said such a thing? What is wrong with me?

Her eyes filled with tears as she looked at her husband and suddenly remembered how tender and transported he'd been at the birth of each child—even, and especially, Stoney.

Maybe I should tear those pages out of my diary, she thought.

Gil's eyes burned; his heart seemed clenched like a fist in his chest, a hard, dangerous, painful fist. Yet when he looked at Irene, there was that futile sense of need. They were standing in the doorway. She was going out. Of course she was going out. She was going out to swim laps, up and down, for a mile, in the pool. It was as if she were swimming out to sea.

He said to her softly, but in a deadly voice: You don't know how much I love you, and I wish I didn't since you obviously don't want me to, but I do, and I wish it so much that one of my persistent fantasies is that when we die we are both cremated and our ashes are mixed together in one beautiful vase, like the vase we bought together in Venice, the one we couldn't afford but bought anyway, remember, perhaps that vase, or maybe something sacred, like the horn of a buffalo, maybe, or our ashes are scattered together in a special place like the top of a mountain, maybe, the one we hiked to in Wyoming, remember, or a lake up north, maybe, just so that our ashes could be together for all time, Irene, for all time. That's what I wish.

No, thought Irene, turning away. I am going to leave those pages exactly as I wrote them.

Riel had nearly finished the volumes of letters. She read each page several times as she came toward the end, and then went backward and forward again. She didn't want the books to end. She spoke the names of the people whose portraits appeared in Catlin's exhibitions: The Constant Walker, Little Stabbing

Chief, Whirling Thunder, Swimmer, Soup, Fire, Sturgeon Head, Wild Sage, Rotten Foot, Blue Medicine, No Heart, The Steep Wind, The Mink, Long Finger Nails, Broken Pot, Mint, Double Walker, Black Drink.

Then she read how smallpox was introduced among the Mandan by a fur trader who stopped at their village with a sick man on board his boat. In the course of two months, nearly all of the Mandan died. Once infected most died within hours. Half of the others shot themselves dead or leapt headfirst off the thirty-foot rock ledges that surrounded their village. She read that the village was one continual howling and whole families were left to decay in their lodges. At last she read how the greatest of warriors, Mahtotohpa, sat in his lodge and witnessed the deaths of his children and wives, but somehow himself lived, and then walked through the village, weeping. He went out and lay on the ledges refusing food or drink, until on the ninth day he crawled back into his family's lodge and covered himself with his robes to die.

Riel put down the book and pulled her covers over her head. She lay still, in darkness, until she could no longer bear her thoughts. Then she got up and went looking for her mother. She searched the house until, at the bottom of the stairs up to her father's studio, she heard her mother talking to him. She started up the steps, but as she got closer and Irene's voice got louder she recognized a certain intimate, joking quality. She edged back down the steps. She never intruded upon the two of them when they were laughing together, talking excitedly over each other, when they sounded happy.

Riel went back into her room and pulled her comforter back over her head. She thought of Mahtotohpa's tragic loyalty and came to a conclusion. In the event of a disaster, she would have to take charge. She would have to find a way to save her family. What she had read convinced her again that anything could happen. All through history, this was proven—the worst imaginable things really did come true.

In the early evening, Irene started to think about how angry she and Gil had made the therapist. The whole episode struck her as hopelessly funny. She went up to Gil's studio, stood in the doorway, and said in a fake-wifey voice, Are you sure I can't be South Korea?

Gil turned to her, already laughing.

Her face, when you said the children's fathers were three other men!

You two aren't serious, Irene mimicked. You are dithering around!

We can't go back to her.

No, we've blown it. We're bad clients.

We're too sick for her.

We're just too fucking hopeless.

They laughed together and held hands as they went down-stairs. Gil sat in the kitchen and they paged through cookbooks until Irene decided on a favorite meal, one they all liked—a Mexican cilantro shrimp and rice dish. Gil ran out for the ingredients. They were low on money, but Gil bought expen-sive wines anyway, three different kinds. That night after the children had gone to sleep, they took the wine bottles, glasses, and ice bucket up to his studio.

Gil wanted to show Irene the portrait—better now. After that disturbing therapy session he had made sweeping changes. Maybe now it was even very good. He knew she was humoring him and didn't want to go up the stairs. Once she was there and seated in the old velveteen armchair, though, she softened and became pensive. He showed her the picture, and he could see by her face she was touched by the intolerable longing in her portrait, and something else. A remanence.

It is masterful, she said at last. One of your best.

Charged suddenly with pleasure, with happiness, he poured the chilled, fragrant, faintly pink-gold wine into her glass and watched her drink it. She smiled. Gil relaxed and let himself be funny and sincere and just a little distancing so that he could feel her, once she was through her second glass, leaning toward him as he praised her. She began talking in the old way, flirting with him, laughing.

She took her clothing off eventually and lay there sipping at the wine. Irene asked to listen to the old cassette tapes he'd played when they first met. He still had them—world music, aboriginal music, desert music, deer dance music, Huichol music. Scriabin, Schubert, Bach. He liked Judy Garland and Etta James. He liked Dan Seals and Dire Straits. Some of the music was irritating, Irene said, as she always said, but by then she was drunk.

Irene lay on her back with her knees drawn up together, tilted neatly to one side. She fell asleep. Her empty wineglass toppled onto the lush dark green blanket as her fingers relaxed. Gil adjusted his lights and continued to paint. Eventually, he put down his brushes, walked over to his wife, and gently teased her knees open. She drew her thighs up, then sighed and they flopped nervelessly apart. Gil stepped back, adjusted his lights to shine starkly between her legs. Her face was thrown into shadow.

He continued to paint as the windows went from black to deep blue. He mixed his favorite colors right on the painting. When dawn turned the windows gray, he cleaned his brushes meticulously, one by one. He removed the panel from the easel and brought it to a corner, draping a small drop cloth over it. He took a can of tomato juice out of his refrigerator and drank it, watching Irene sleep. Once he'd finished, he got out a bottle of orange juice, four aspirins, a glass of water. He put these on a tray and set it silently next to Irene. At last, he unfolded a soft cotton blanket and covered her. She shifted in her sleep, licked her lips, and frowned. Gil could hear the children downstairs now, and went out quietly, to get their breakfasts.

The temperature dropped, one of those drastic 50 degree plunges that enervate and exhilarate the body all at once. Irene said she'd take the car out because it was important to run the engine during deep cold. Gil made an appointment for her car, so she could get a new battery. The online temperature was -34 but school had not been canceled and Irene left an hour early—she'd pick the children up when she'd finished writing in the little room at the bank.

She wore her white down coat, padded fleece mitts, sheepskin-lined boots, a scarf to breathe through. The streets were empty and there was a mist of exhaust in the air. She walked into the bank lobby, past the coin-to-cash machine, and around to the back. There were no customers, and the few tellers on duty were softly murmuring and laughing. The stairs were set into a rounded white ceremonial-looking wall, and the desk with its attendant was at the bottom. Janice greeted her by name, took her key, and went into the closet behind her desk to match the key.

Staying warm? she said as she opened the vault. That was what everybody said.

Doing my best, said Irene. That was how everyone replied.

December 5, 2007

BLUE NOTEBOOK

C old out, but I want the hurt because I hurt. Too much wine last night. My face feels plastered crudely onto the bones of my face. Bones of a fish. Maybe if I convince Gil that he is not the father of our children he will let us go. Just let us walk right out of the house.

There were two couches in the TV room, one slightly behind the other one. Florian was watching his father as his father watched television. He had been told that it was a family night, and he was therefore forbidden to sit alone in his room at the computer. So he sat with Riel. But the two of them were not watching television, they were watching their father laugh, eat popcorn, sip wine. From time to time, Gil stopped doing these other things and said to Stoney, who sat stiffly beside him, Where is your mom?

There was a movie coming on and he wanted her to see the beginning. There was an empty place on the couch for her, and an empty wineglass set next to a tawny brown bottle that slowly acquired a dull glaze of perspiration as it sat, waiting.

Irene's car pulled up behind the house; the door slammed. Gil told Stoney to run and tell her where we were.

Stoney, who liked to do errands, shot off. Gil looked expectantly at the screen and said, It's coming on. Florian and Riel sat on the back couch with their arms folded. And now Riel watched Florian watch their father instead of the screen. Riel touched Florian's arm as their mother walked into the room, glowing with cold.

Look, said Florian, quiet, she is approaching the Schwarz-schild radius.

He had explained this theory to Riel the day before, so she knew that the Schwarzschild radius was the imagined point at which the light reflected off a body loses more and more energy as it struggles to escape a black hole's phenomenal gravity.

Their mother's face went taut as she tried to back out of the room, and then brittle and pleasant as she realized there was no alternative to sitting down beside her husband. He poured her a glass of wine and her skin transferred its luminous energy to what she now drank.

She has fallen within the radius, Florian whispered to Riel.

Riel also remembered that Florian had described this proximity as the distance, or point of no return, from which nothing, not even a shadow, can be retrieved.

The Workout Barbie bag was clearly inadequate. Riel had badgered Florian to bring a survival book home from the high school library and at last he had, a red book, *Prepare for Disaster*. Remember, said Florian, tossing the book to Riel. She had told him that she was going to insert him into her escape plan, which she knew would make everything more complicated. It was like starting over. Now that she had professional guidelines, she realized that her plans were weak. She would have starved within a month and been faced with a terrible choice—to eat her dogs or be eaten by them. Both she and they would have reverted to feral creatures and the normal taboos of species sentiment would have dissolved. The Mandan had eaten their dogs, but Riel knew this was beyond her. She knew that she would rather they eat her. In that way, she would respectfully return her body to the wild. Better not to face that choice at all.

She read about the possibility of a dirty bomb scenario, in which it would be death to venture outdoors. If survival involved a gas mask, then clearly she was doomed along with almost everyone else in the city. If it was a simple case of outlasting radiation, though, her revised plan was to duct tape not only Florian but her whole entire family, together with the dogs of course, into the large basement closet. It would shortly become a hellhole. Still, she would do her best. Riel knew that her mother had saved at least a year's worth of plastic sauce containers from their favorite Chinese takeout, and these she secretly placed in a corner of the closet along with several rolls of toilet paper. That would help. She also needed wet wipes, water, and food. The water was simple—Riel took the gallon milk jugs from the recycling bin. She filled the jugs with water, brought them down to the closet, and covered them with a rug. Now that she had decided to save her entire family, it looked like she would need an endless amount of water. She was in it for the long haul. As for food, she pilfered like a squirrel. She hoarded Baggies of nuts and cereal—high-calorie foods, as was advised. She brought these down and stuck them in a plastic bagel keeper. She promised herself to do one little thing every day, to ensure the well-being of her family in the advent of doomsday.

As the closet became organized into a lifesaving shelter, Riel had thought she would feel safer, but the opposite occurred. She dreamed surging floods, tanks as big as houses, black helicopters raining down fire, and, the worst, hydrophobia. She dreamed that all of the dogs in the world went mad and tore their owners to pieces. When she woke, her face was wet with tears and she could hardly breathe. Each sick animal in her dream had developed a red mark on its ear. Riel went straight to the dogs and looked at their ears. When she saw that they were unmarked, she buried her face in their dry, wintry fur. Their hot, rank breath flowed over her, comforting her, and she thought that she had really better develop the mental toughness described by the author of the book. Breathe from the gut, she counseled herself.

Irene walked into Louise's studio and sat down on her purple velvet couch. The cloth was old and shiny in places and smelled of Louise's big roan greyhound, rescued from the dog tracks. A salty, intimate smell. The ceiling was a seventeenth-century sky surrounded by fat, spoiled cherubs holding golden garlands. There were dozens of bright canvases, half finished, finished. The greyhound crouched elegantly at Louise's feet. Irene had simply driven over, walked in without warning.

She said nothing, just looked at Louise.

You didn't answer my calls, said Louise.

Irene was wearing the gauzy scarf Louise had given her for her birthday.

Look, said Louise. He called me up and told me about the party after I painted Stoney's ceiling. It was part of the plan—his heart's desire project, he called it. Later on, he wanted me to make sure you didn't come home until the party was all in place. There was something off. He wanted me to follow you and to find out where you'd been all day.

Irene's face burned.

I'm sorry. I thought he'd get somebody else to follow you so I figured I'd take the job because whatever you did—not that you did anything—but I mean . . . who knows, whatever. I wasn't going to tell. You're my sister.

Irene searched Louise's face.

Did you tell him you're my sister?

No.

Irene's face cleared. She took a deep breath.

I'm going to leave him.

Louise looked down. Her dog's keen muzzle slipped into her hand.

I don't know how to get out.

Then you need a lawyer.

Irene nodded her head and felt like she might throw up. She slid sideways and slumped over, head on her knees.

Louise sat down and put her arm around her.

How about some water? Tea?

I need red wine.

It's morning.

Louise tightened her arms around Irene and the dog paced around and around the two women on the couch. The dog stopped and leaned against Louise. Irene put her hand on the dog's brow. The idea of a full glass of deep burgundy, peppery and restorative, only faded a little.

I can have it later, Irene thought. She sat up.

If something happens, will you take care of my kids?

Shut up! People get divorced all the time.

Louise?

Okay. Tell the lawyer.

Irene nodded. She couldn't say it, but she knew she was destroying a world. A little culture. It was the known and safe way of behaving in the family. All the rituals, wrong or sick, it didn't matter, good or bad, would be useless. All the strategies. They knew the familiar treacheries, but now they would be open to new dangers.

People do it all the time, she said to Louise. I don't know how. I don't even know where to start.

With the lawyer, remember?

Oh, yes.

And another thing, Irene. You have to quit drinking.

Irene nodded.

I'll think about doing that, she carefully said.

For three nights, Irene kept herself sober. Every time she wanted to take a drink, she poured herself a glass of water. I've never peed so much in my whole life, she said to herself in the bathroom mirror. I don't even know if this is possible. She went downstairs. She poured herself another glass of water. She waited for Gil to read the diary and react. But every night he just fell asleep on the couch by the magnificent fireplace with the television endlessly on CNN. When he looked about to nod off, she went outside with the children all bundled up and walked the dogs in the cold. Returning, they watched their father through the window. They looked at him fondly, as if he were an animal in a zoo. A dangerous animal lovable in sleep. An animal whose fur invited petting, but who might eat them if they did.

They tiptoed past him when it got too cold to stay outside. They slept curled around their mother, all together, upstairs on the amazingly thick carpets.

George Catlin's work was not appreciated in the United States, so he had his entire collection packed up and put aboard a ship bound for London, where he would exhibit and give lectures. He left his family behind with great reluctance, but he took along a strange prize. A cage aboard the ship contained two grizzly bears he'd caught when they were, as he said, "no larger than my foot." Now the cubs were nearly full grown. He planned to exhibit them, too.

The two grizzlies, whose normal range would cover hundreds of miles, and who are certainly among the most powerful beings on earth, were confined on the top deck of a sailing ship in an iron cage the size of a small bedroom. If the bears hadn't gone mad before they were put aboard the ship, the voyage surely drove them insane. During a storm, the misery and terror of the animals was such that they seemed about to break the ship itself apart. They rammed themselves from side to side in the cube and gnawed the bars of their cages until their teeth broke. One managed on a calm day to swipe off a sailor's nose with a clever blow. It was even worse for the bears in London, where they were surrounded at all times by crowds of people who pelted them with stones to hear them bawl and roar. Catlin wrote of their agony with amusement, even an attempt at irony, contending that the bears owed him "four years maintenance" as well as some remuneration for the sights they'd been privileged to see on their travels. At last, with light discernment, he said that "from the continual crowds around them, to which they had the greatest repugnance, they seemed daily to pine, until one died of exceeding disgust . . . the other with similar symptoms, added to loneliness perhaps, and despair, in a few months afterwards."

Irene had written her thoughts about this incident on note cards. The bears died of the disgust of being constantly looked at. The more Irene thought about this, the more such a death made sense. It seemed reasonable. It seemed that people had forgotten what a terrible thing it was to be looked at, and then she began to imagine that in giving away her image, to be looked at and looked at, she was somehow killing herself of disgust. She wrote this down on a note card but then tore it up. Three days is a long time, she wrote on another card. Long enough. I have proved that I do not need to drink.

Once she poured the glass of wine she had craved, the tension of proving herself dissipated. Warmed, loosened, relieved, Irene took the bottle down to her desk with a sandwich. It was late afternoon and entirely appropriate. Later, she could have a glass of scotch with Gil and more wine with dinner, and it would still be entirely appropriate. As she sipped wine, she could write, which was common, to write while sipping wine. She did not have to pick up anyone today. A relaxed and almost tearful happiness flowed into her. She'd hung quilts on the whitewashed walls and the colors and patterns calmed her. She had a calico star quilt, a Tennessee Rose of Sharon, a crazy quilt, and an old Bear Claw pattern. She looked at each of them with affection. She loved her office the way an animal loves its cave. She nibbled on her sandwich.

Water gurgled through the pipes as the dishwasher completed its cycle. The dogs' nails clicked across the wooden floors overhead as they paced to the windows to check on passersby. The dogs assessed those who came into their territory and either barked a warning or decided there was no harm. The house was surrounded by oak trees and sometimes the dull, muted roar of wind reverberated through their roots. Irene could hear the hollow rush of energy behind the limestone blocks of the foundation. All at once, in the sweet grip of the alcohol, she could feel their blind power. She could feel it steal into her. They had been secretly looking out for her. She opened her diary and continued writing.

December 10, 2007

RED DIARY

L ove is difficult to distinguish from symmetry. Gil was an artist and I liked art. Gil talked. I listened. I went to one of Gil's openings—a big deal. I'd wangled the invitation. I lied and told him that I was an artist's model. He lied and told me that he needed to hire a model. I looked at his paintings, all landscapes, and smiled at him. Gil said that he would pay me. I needed the money.

I began to sit for him in his warehouse studio. At first I was shy, but the way his eyes rested on me, the quality of his attention, was both neutral and sexual. Sometimes he would get very close to me, stare at my hair, my skin, my nipples. But he did not touch me. We'd listen to music while he painted. He liked complex sitar music—dot-Indian music, we called it, and we both liked our own feather-Indian music, too—we liked Northern Cree, Carlos Nakai, Black Lodge.

I kept modeling, getting paid, so that I could stay in school and become a historian. I wanted to be a historian because I notice patterns. Symmetry is very powerful with me. As it turned out, Gil needed symmetry too. We were hooked by likeness, or a likeness. Then my likeness. More symmetry: we were both raised by single mothers. We both hardly knew our fathers. Both mixed-bloods, Native, even had Cree and Chippewa blood in common. Both wanted children. Both arguers. Readers. Both drinkers. The first time we had sex, we were drunk. The first time we had sex when we were not drunk, it was so surprising, so moving, so intimate, that we fell immediately in love. We both had a taboo about intimate awareness. It was equally intimidating to us both.

The idea of symmetry was so powerful that for many years I did not understand the design had warped. I tried to keep the romance going by thinking of symmetrical things to do—things we'd done in the beginning.

I arranged for us to do these things all over again. Picnics. Birth. People always use old tropes to try and stay in love. We'd been in Paris our first year. So Paris beckoned again. A crooked, agile finger all the way from across the Atlantic.

The hotel lobby had exposed black ceiling beams snugly plastered in between. You could see the entrance of a stone cellar that once had belonged to a monastery. Our hotel was described as luxurious, but our room was a murky brocaded recess underneath other expressive, wormholed beams, which seemed to descend lower every morning.

The year was 2000. Florian was six and Riel four. I wanted another baby because that's what people do when they don't know they are falling out of love. Sometimes it brings them back together, and they don't know they were ever in danger. I wanted to love Gil and had the confused idea that I'd fall in love with him all over again by falling in love with his baby. Gil did not want another child to compete with, however, and he suspected that I'd stopped using birth control. He was avoiding me. Wouldn't touch me. In Paris! I'd expected place to overcome all of this. People expect a lot from Paris.

Catlin lost his wife and his son there. Many Indians are buried in Paris. It's hard for Paris to satisfy everyone.

One afternoon, I declined drinks with Gil's art dealer. I was tired of walking. I needed to complain. I would ask Our Lady of Notre-Dame to provide my husband an erection. After all, the cathedral was constructed on the site of an ancient temple to Jupiter, and the exact same thing had been going on for a millennium or two in this very spot. Only the candles and the penises changed. The hearts of women were the same.

There was a crowd, as always. I dropped my coins into the little brass box. I lighted a taper off the flame of a burning votive and sat in a little wooden chair at the feet of Mary. She was not the original statue. That one had been destroyed in the revolution. This Virgin was fairly insipid. Still, I prayed, to the building itself, which seemed to have sprung with immense power out of the earth. I had walked toward it from the Ile St. Louis, and the back view was both lovely and grotesque, strangely sexual, splayed and buttressed like a couple of alien creatures preparing to mate.

I crossed myself and turned away. Walking out, I passed a man kneeling in the back of the church, a man somewhat older than me, and possibly drunk. He was unshaven and looked as though he had been weeping. He got up and followed me out of the cathedral, and then down behind the cathedral, onto the island—an old cow pasture now some of the world's most expensive real estate, to a café called Le Flore en l'Ile, just over the short bridge and lighted a soft gold.

I went into the café, took a chair beside the window, and ordered from a brisk waiter. The man from the cathedral seated himself one table away. The waiter came back swiftly with my coffee and poured a precise amount of frothy, heated milk into my cup. He turned with a military flourish toward the man from the cathedral, who stared at me with startling eyes. When I glanced his way, he gestured at the empty chair, which was tucked against my little table. The waiter stopped between us and shook the chair, eyeing me significantly as if to say, Shall I remove this chair and foil him? I looked back at the man from the cathedral, and remained motionless. The waiter shrugged and took his hand off the chair. He nodded as the man spoke his order in a low, scratchy voice. Then the waiter left us, and the man from the cathedral walked over and sat down.

This is awful, Irene thought. She put down the pen and diary. The wine was nearly gone. I am enjoying the invention of this man too much, this romantic and world-weary sort of man. I forgot the weary, sexy lines at the corners of his eyes. I'll have to put them in the next diary entry.

She replaced her red diary in its hiding place and went up-stairs. It was her night to cook and she made a soup of lentils, cream, garlic, and nutmeg. There was bread, a salad of romaine lettuce with little pumpernickel croutons, dried cranberries, and goat cheese. She kept drinking and grew cheerful. Nothing seemed to affect her. Everyone ate calmly, and the evening pro-gressed as any evening might in a normal family. The children made the perfect trifecta of dishes/homework/bed—and Gil was caught up with some political drama on the news.

Irene could not stop thinking about the imaginary man who had followed her into the café in Paris. She couldn't stop sentences, phrases, descriptions, from entering her mind. Instead of reading herself to sleep, she crept downstairs and continued writing.

The man got up from his chair and shambled over to sit across from me. He was an unnoticeable person, really, until I saw his eyes. After I saw his eyes, I noticed everything about him, as did most women, I suppose. Eyes like that are a kind of curse for a man, I would think. It is hard to get past that sort of gaze. Having it would be nice at first, like being extremely wealthy, but your life might end badly if you didn't learn how to control your worst impulses. You could die of gluttony and drugs. You could die of sex. Things might seem easy but they really wouldn't be. It looked to me as though this man was on the other side of having suffered some of those realizations. He wasn't drunk, though, or at least not anymore, and although he had that slightly awkward, lurching walk, he was lucid and dignified in his manner. He seemed merely curious about me, once he sat down. He spoke English and said that I looked like an American. He asked if I liked Paris. I said that I liked Paris and he asked why I had come to Notre-Dame. I told him the truth, that I had come to pray to have a child. Then I asked him why he had come to the cathedral. Before he answered, the waiter brought his coffee, and the man stirred sugar into it and drank a little. I thought that he was going to tell me a lie or say something ridiculous. But he told me that he had stopped believing in God when he was a teenage boy, and that had not changed. Then, one month ago, his older brother had been killed in a car accident and since then he had been unable to sleep. If he did manage to fall asleep, he said, he was always awakened by his brother, who had been a priest. He said the visits were disturbing because his brother had died without confessing his sins. Now that he was dead, the brother wanted to confess his sins. Every night he spoke in great detail about the sins he had committed as a priest.

The man put up his hand as if he knew what I was thinking. He kept talking.

I hasten to say that these sins are extremely boring, small sins, very foolish little sins, the sort of thing that I for instance would not be much troubled by. My brother was always the more sensitive one, but these sins, ah!

He smiled at me, rubbing his face.

I want to say to him, Brother! If you had to sin why didn't you really sin? Why didn't you commit a sin worth confessing? You are consumed now in your afterlife with trivialities. I wish that you were repenting of some great passion. That might be worth staying awake for!

Anyway, the man shrugged, my brother will probably come to the end of things. He can't go on forever. Someday I will actually sleep. I came here to pray—even though I do not believe in God, I am superstitious—I prayed that my brother be absolved of his sins so that I can rest.

It is an unusual request, I said.

Yours is not so unusual, he said in a gentle way.

I said that I had become aware of that while praying. I asked if he had children.

One daughter. But her mother and I . . . he made a little stick-breaking gesture . . . still we have affection for each other. And my daughter, a joy. You have . . . He paused.

I have a husband. He is out with friends. I flung my hand toward the river. My throat hurt.

I have to go.

May I walk with you? I live in that direction.

I took some money from my purse but he closed my hand on the money and laid his own on the table.

You are beautiful, he said, looking at me frankly.

I was close enough to catch the scent of him, a dusky animal undertone.

Just a studio, with big long windows and an old worn table, a tiny kitchen made with blue and white tiles. The little lamps beside the bed had rose-colored shades. There were feminine touches, but no sign of a woman. A large stereo and racks of CDs and more CDs scattered all around on the carpets, the leather couch. He stacked them up to make space for us to lie together, then the pile went clattering across the floor, and he laughed. There were several computers against one wall. Posters and programs stacked or propped on chairs. He was a music critic, probably. Or just a lover of music. He sat naked in a kitchen chair. We rocked the chair across the slick floor until it was wedged up against the sink. We stood against the door of a closet and lay on the couch. There were stacks of books, too. Art books. One book of Bonnard reproductions. When I looked at a Bonnard the next day in the Centre Pompidou, I think I wept. There was a big old bathtub, deep. Afterward he held me for an hour and I memorized details of the room. The muted blue figures of birds and leaves in the drapes. Magazines underneath a table leg to level it. The soft cream yarn of the blanket. A mirror that bounced traffic light back into the streets. I knew that someday I'd write it down. We got up. We put our clothing on. I just left. I did not take his phone number. I did not kiss him, either, before I left. Sometimes, when I look at Stoney, I wish I had kissed him. I wish I could thank him.

On the way back from his apartment, in the cab, I was appalled, mystified, at peace. Like a baby, it made me happy to have smashed something. I didn't think of it as the symmetry, as the love. There was a drifting, humming noise in my head. But when I got back to the room, there was Gil, worried, though I'd left a note. The air now was very dark.

I told him simply that I had gone to Notre-Dame to light candles there, and to pray for a baby. I was smiling as I said this, and I could tell that Gil was taken by the romance of the story. I could tell he felt sorry for me, too, so nakedly showing my need. He put his hand on my shoulder in a brotherly way, and then bent over. His hand tightened and he drew me closer. He kissed me and drew his body around me and lifted me onto the bed. He became aroused so suddenly that I was confused. I had done nothing. Maybe it was all that Catholic training, I thought, and almost laughed. The power of Notre-Dame! A moment later, I knew that it was the scent of the man with green eyes that my husband was reacting to, the scent of our lovemaking had aroused him. This was what Gil did to make me fall out of love with him. It happened the night Stoney was made, conceived, not born. This was the beginning—I pushed Gil away. A tremendous loneliness enveloped me, from then on, whenever Gil touched me.

Irene put down the diary. Her shoulders and hips ached. Sleep itched her eyes and her scalp had tightened painfully, a constricting cap. She hid it and was nearly upstairs before she remembered that even while writing she'd thought she might rip the pages out. But why should I? She sleepily continued walking up the stairs, hand on the smooth, curved cherrywood banister. Gil wanted me in relation to another man's desire. Even he didn't know that, but it was true. It was why he magnified my sexuality in the paintings. It was why he teased the viewer with my image. He was competitive. He needed to possess something other men wanted, which is actually quite an ordinary thing for a man to do. But of course, that left me entirely out of the equation. A memory snagged at her as she passed into the velvet dark of the bedroom. A performance she'd seen. A small innovative theater in Minneapolis once staged an extraordinary rape scene from *Rashomon*. A mirror lay on the ground. A man fell brutally upon the mirror and fucked his own image. The victim watched him from the shadows.

I was no victim, of course; I was passive. I was vain. But then he fell on the mirror and made love to his own image every day, every night, the image he had created of a woman desired by other men. I was not supposed to be this woman, Irene wrote the next day, miserably sick, hungover. I disappoint myself.

Gil stood high in the solid, graceful house, and looked out into the tops of the oak trees. He didn't want to go downstairs; he didn't want to read his wife's diary; he didn't want to be an angry person or to beg her to love him. He wanted to keep working on the portrait of Irene, which was improving steadily with all of the shocks she had given him. They all yielded, eventually. This one would, too. But at some point, he was going to have to read the diary in order to find out if she'd really meant what she said about the children's various fathers. It was too outrageous. Absurd. Too vicious. Still, it gave him satisfaction to think how she had disquieted the therapist.

Irene called from the bottom of the stairs. She had changed her mind about parties, it seemed. They were going out that night. They had to dress. He said that he was coming, and waited until he heard her running water for her bath. Her eternal, self-indulgent, infuriating soaks.

While she was in the bathtub, he went downstairs and quickly pulled her diary from its hiding place. Once he read the first few lines, dread lurched through him. He saw where this was going. He skimmed in sick rapidity over the first two men and then her writing slowed and he was with her, and with that man in the café. He could see them. He could see everything. When it stopped, he dug his fingers so hard into his face he drew blood. He dropped the diary and started up the stairs. Halfway, he collapsed and gripped the rail. He forced himself to choke the air in and out, but his breath kept popping from his chest as if he was being dealt huge, invisible blows.

What is it? said Irene from the top of the stairs. Are you all right?

Fine, said Gil. Let me sit here. Catch my breath.

Irene went back into the bathroom and stood in front of the mirror putting on her makeup. Her foundation was called Latte Love. She smoothed it carefully up the violet circles under her eyes. She dusted her eyelids with blush, then drew lines along her lashes with cake eyeliner. She used just a bit of mascara on her lashes and brows. She rubbed a plum stain of gloss onto her lips. Blotted with a bit of Kleenex. Finally, she chose a scent from the line of bottles Gil had given her, a fragrance that was not flowery, but bitter, like some exotic, hillside undergrowth.

Are you ready? she called. He was now in the downstairs bathroom.

No.

Ten minutes later, she knocked on the bathroom door.

We'll be late.

I cut myself shaving, said Gil.

She sat with Stoney, reading a book, until finally Gil was ready.

Gil was holding her coat when she came down the stairs. The babysitter had been playing crazy eights with Riel, but she quit and went upstairs to take over reading to Stoney. Irene glanced at Gil and something in his weary surrender registered and pulled at her. She spoke brightly.

I'm going to be with the handsomest man at the party.

Riel, who had been waiting for her father to say this, looked at her mother strangely and walked upstairs. Gil stepped behind Irene and held her coat open. He knew that he looked like a man who'd been mortally punched in the guts, or a flu victim who'd thrown up for days. He looked like a desolate fool, a haunted idiot, a husband.

The door slammed. Their parents were gone. Curled with Stoney in Stoney's bed, the babysitter was reading *Grandfather Twilight* over and over.

How many times can Grandfather give that pearl to the sea? said Riel.

Florian and Riel began playing Halo 3 on the secret Xbox that Florian had inherited from a rich kid at school. The box had crashed, and correcting the red ring of death was beyond him.

Gramps will give that pearl to the sea forever, said Florian. Or until the Charm Quark falls asleep. Florian locked the laser gun on Riel's Spartan and blew it up. I just totally owned you, he said. Let's quit.

Florian and Riel went downstairs to the kitchen. Florian opened the low cupboard where Gil kept the bottles of wine, neatly set on scalloped shelves. Florian drew out a bottle.

Côtes du Rhone. Whatever.

Do you think they'll notice? said Riel.

Florian looked at her from under his eyebrows. He took a corkscrew out of the drawer.

Let's go up on the roof.

They grabbed coats, hats, mittens, a rug, and crept up through the hallway. The babysitter's voice droned sweetly. She was eighteen. She would spend the rest of the evening tidying a little and then writing a college paper on her laptop, downstairs. Florian and Riel slipped through Gil's studio to the ladder that led up onto the roof. The trapdoor was hard to lift. Florian stuck the bottle in the waist of his jeans and they managed to force the trapdoor up and aside. They crept out, across the flat tar space of the roof, to the great bank of brick chimneys, where they put down the rug. The night was freezing and the wind stiff. Florian opened the bottle and each of them tipped it back. Then Florian pulled out a joint and took two hits. Riel took a little puff. Over the roof, reaching up over three stories, the oaks twisted and creaked. The back of the house looked over the 394 and 94 interchanges, the sculpture garden, the basilica, and past that the city, solid and steadily shining.

What's light again?

Light's odd, said Florian, there's nothing to it, no mass, yet it is bent by gravity. It acts like a wave. It acts like a particle. Understanding the two as one is humanly ungraspable. So do not think you are alone. Light hits something solid, it will not go through it. Light's energy. Do you think Mom and Dad will get a divorce?

I don't know, said Riel. Maybe.

I think they will. I think they hate each other. Mom's light, though. Dad's a neutron star.

What's that again?

You know, a collapsing star spins faster. Becoming dense, pulling everything in. She's having trouble breaking out.

The Schwarzschild radius.

Yeah! You got it! Florian took another drink and handed the bottle to Riel. He was always happy when Riel remembered something he had told her. She moved a little closer, shivering.

Here. Florian took his heavy knitted scarf off and draped it around Riel. She tucked it up to her neck.

I'm gonna have a cigarette, he said. But you can only inhale one time, okay? I don't want to get you hooked on these.

Weed did not affect Riel, she thought. Or maybe just a little. Everything seemed good. Supernormal. The sky over Minneapolis glowed orange and violet. The colored band at the top of the Target Center slowly changed from red to green, for Christmas.

What will they do with us?

Charm Quark, I hope he doesn't get him, said Florian, blowing smoke in a stream that whipped past Riel's face.

I heard Mom talking to a lawyer.

No shit, that's encouraging.

I think it's better if we stay the way we are, I mean, we know how to deal with them, you know?

I see your point. Have you made any friends yet, by the way?

No.

They started laughing.

No, said Florian. Tienes *any* amigos? Not a single fucking pal?

No solo yo. Get out the violins.

We're gonna have to find you a peer group, Top Quark.

I don't care.

And so the lion ate Pierre. You do care. It's lonely out there.

They both drank. The bottle was half gone. After Florian finished his cigarette, he relighted the joint and took another hit. Riel took one, too, then dizzily waved it away.

Yeah, Florian said. That's all we know. It's all dark matter. Ninety-five percent of it. We have no fucking conclusion here.

What kind of particle are you?

A worthy question, Top Quark. Let me think.

Florian smoked for a while, looking out over the constant motion of the lights.

Okay, I got it. I was going to say I am a tau, but no, I think I'm an unobserved particle. I'm only hypothetical. An electron gets a selectron. For every tau there is a stau. Florian sang, For every muon there is a smuon.

A smuon?

They started laughing, tried to stop. Florian started up again every time Riel said, Smuon?

For real. Smuon.

Florian got up and walked to the edge of the roof. For every muon there is a smuon! He sang and then pirouetted against the sky like a dancer in an old black-and-white movie.

Riel laughed and said, Come on back, Florian. Come back. But he balanced on the edge of the roof. Dancing back and forth, he waved his arms. The roof did not drop straight off. There was an old-fashioned mansard band that slanted sharply down and was roofed in slate shingles that clattered off sometimes, but broke only if they hit the steps. They were so heavy they could brain a person, Mom had said.

Please, Florian. Riel was stuck in the center of a whirl of lights.

Florian, please! she yelled. Come on, I'm gonna shit my pants!

Florian put his foot up as if he were going to step over the edge, but pivoted back, still dancing. When he reached Riel, she grabbed his arm hard and was silent.

What? You gotta go?

She said nothing.

Florian sat beside her. He lighted another cigarette. They finished the bottle. Riel's teeth were chattering.

Come on, said Florian. Talk to me.

Riel still couldn't talk.

I'm sorry, said Florian at last.

Please, said Riel in a whisper. Don't ever do that. It's lonely out here, Smuon.

Florian patted her arm.

Okay, I'm not a smuon, maybe, a smuon is too crazy. The W boson has an unobserved partner called a Wino. I'm just a Wino.

Not funny now.

Okay, I know. I'll be a WIMP. That's a weakly interacting massive particle.

That's better, maybe. I'm freezing. Let's go play more Halo.

Florian stood up with the empty bottle in his hand and suddenly cocked his arm back. With a graceful arc of effort he hurled the bottle over the trees. A moment later they heard it crash in the street. He looked at Riel until she finally nodded and said, Nice.

Okay, Top Quark, I'll play you, said Florian. Prepare for wastage.

Ha ha. Riel climbed down the ladder. You're the wasted one.

I still have razor reflexes.

Dull razors, dull noncutting razors.

You're not so razorly yourself, Top Quark, you missed that step.

I'm deadly hungry.

We'll get food. Your last meal before execution, little sister.

Your last meal, Puon.

Puon! They made their way down the stairs, past the babysitter, laughing.

You two are stoned, she said.

Don't tell, O beautiful pearl sea woman, said Florian, grinning crookedly.

She smiled and went back to typing on her laptop.

Florian and Riel wove into the kitchen and piled food on a cookie sheet. They went back upstairs to Florian's room, ate and played Halo until the grass and wine wore off and Riel got sleepy. She stumbled off to her own bed, across the hall. Florian followed her after a moment. Riel had flopped down on top of her bedspread. Florian took a blanket from the bottom of the bed, arranged it over his sister. Then he went back to his room, sat before his computer, and typed in his father's name.

That night, after they returned from the party and Irene went to sleep, Gil was agitated, wired, so he went up to his studio to look at the painting of Irene. The studio was freezing, as if someone had left the windows open. He put an old sweater on and stood, staring. He had done her vulva well, he thought. There was goodness and sincerity in the brushstrokes. Of course, she'd been drunk, she hadn't known, she hadn't seen this portrait. But even after what he'd read, what she'd done, her betrayal, he didn't slash the painting. He didn't do anything but deepen the shadow on her face. He believed that he wasn't capable of not loving Irene, but he did think of sharpening his paintbrush and driving it like a stake into his heart.

He had looked at the Lucretia so many times that he could feel her heartbreak form on his own face. His eyes widened and filled. His mouth opened slightly. Yes. He understood.

He sat down heavily. It wouldn't work. He probably couldn't generate enough force or the right trajectory to kill himself, but what a poetic ending. It seemed irresistible, and he started sharpening his longest and most expensive brush with an X-Acto knife. The sharpening took a long time and when he stabbed the point into each palm, it drew blood. He let the blood seep out, then he pressed his hands together until both were uniformly red. He carefully signed the painting with the prints of his hands.

It was the last portrait he would paint of her. His blood signature would darken and fix itself into the painting and become worth a lot of money, in time.

Drifting up from the bottom of sleep, Irene could feel some-one watching her. When she got near the surface, she knew it was Riel. She was not startled when she opened her eyes and Riel was at the bedside motionless in the gray night. She hadn't changed into her pajamas but was wearing saggy jeans and a striped sweater. Her hair hung ragged around her ears and her face was a still blur. Her eyes were so deeply set that Irene couldn't tell at first if they were closed or open. But then a car passed, muffled in the new snow, and glare from its headlamps caromed across the ceiling and walls, briefly sharpening Riel's features. Riel was staring calmly at Irene. Irene stared back at her. The weight of her daughter's gaze was unbearable.

Irene rose without waking Gil, took Riel's hand, and walked her back to her own bed. As soon as she was lying beneath the puffy blue comforter, Riel closed her eyes and breathed evenly. She seemed to have sunk immediately into heavy sleep. Irene sat with Riel a few moments, then silently left the room. Passing Florian's door, she noticed the faint crack of ghostly light from underneath. Thinking that he'd forgotten to turn off his computer, she opened the door and entered.

Florian was sitting at his desk, facing into the glare. Startled, he clicked the picture he'd been looking at off the screen, but there was another behind that and yet another behind that one. Irene approached. At first glance, she thought that Florian was looking at pornography. But when she got up close she realized that the pictures he was rapidly closing off the screen were Gil's early portraits of her.

Florian turned from the screen. Mom?

Go to bed, said Irene.

Florian put the computer to sleep. Irene stood behind him, hugged him before he got into his bed. For the first time in years, she hadn't drunk at a party. She could smell the wine on Florian's breath.

I was so young when your father painted those, she said. Please don't look at them anymore.

I understand. I won't anymore, said Florian.

Irene stepped closer to the bed. She took Florian's desk chair and sat down.

You've been drinking.

Florian did not show his surprise. Yes, he said. I do that from time to time.

Irene nodded. I wish you wouldn't.

I wish you wouldn't, too, said Florian. His face gleamed in the light from the door. He raised himself on one elbow. He was slender and powerful in the black T-shirt.

Irene looked down at her hands. Her hair fell across her face and she composed her features before she pushed the strands back and looked at her son.

Have you been drinking for a long time?

Just a couple of years.

What about Riel?

Her? No. She's way young.

You are too. Why do you look at the paintings?

Florian turned over on his back and groaned. Mom. He

stared at the ceiling. Mom. Okay. I look at them because you loved each other once upon a time. And I was there. I start by looking at the ones where I was a baby. But then sometimes the others . . . some are ugly, some are beautiful.

Maybe you can just look at the last kind.

I don't know why you let him do the others. Florian breathed quickly now. You should have made him quit. Exerted some control. I don't know why you fake him out, why you don't stand up to him. Why you can't just leave and take us with you. Why you didn't leave when I was little. Why?

The last word was harsh, a jagged cry.

Irene cast about for something to say. Florian's expression hardened until he was staring at his mother with contempt. Irene saw a starkly handsome version of Gil, keen as a blade.

You're weak. You're a weakly interacting mom person. A WIMP. Florian gave Irene a false smile. Don't cry. He changed his voice to an insinuating whine. You'll be okay. We'll just put a little ice on that bruise. I mean, ice in that drink.

Irene stood up and began to back from the room.

Sorry, Mom, said Florian in a cold, bored voice. Why don't you just have another drink and go to bed?

The next morning, Irene found her diary splayed on the floor and knew that Gil had read it and then dropped it without a thought to its binding. That was something—but he hadn't done anything, not a thing else. What was he waiting for? What else could she do? How far could she go?

Please let me go, she scrawled on the next blank page. She left the diary where it was, out in the open, knowing that he would never read it again.

You know, said Irene, later on that morning, I think that we should talk to Florian and Riel about the pictures that you have painted of me. The sexual ones. She was subdued. The way Florian had spoken to her left her beaten and bewildered. She kept thinking back to when he was little, the long ago way he had collapsed and held her knees every time she dropped him off at nursery school. How she'd had to peel him away. How she'd sat in her car every time after, her eyes full of tears. And now she wondered, Why did I do that? Why didn't I keep him with me every minute?

We should talk to them, to Florian, she said again.

I'm sorry, said Gil. He wouldn't look at her. I don't see why. Until they ask.

They won't ask.

They won't see the paintings.

They're online.

It probably would not occur . . .

Yes, it would. I'm sure it has. The children will see them, Gil. I think we should talk about them. Maybe we should see that therapist again. I just called. She had a cancellation.

I don't want to. I didn't like her.

She didn't like us.

Can that be good?

Even if she doesn't like us, there are certain things we should work out.

Before we separate? We're not going to do that. I'm not leaving. You're not leaving, said Gil. No one here gets out alive.

What does that mean?

It's just a line from a song.

11 A.M. December 13. The therapist sat in her gray chair, composed and pleasant. She was neutral, which they read as dislike. They could both feel it. It seemed to Gil that the therapist found him, especially, distasteful.

That's a lovely blouse, he said to her. A very nice color on you.

Thank you, said the therapist. I wonder why you find it necessary to compliment me.

I'm trying to woo you, said Gil. I'm trying to get you on my side so I can save my family.

The therapist nearly smiled, but caught herself and leaned back, impassive.

Do you think that's my job?

Sort of, said Gil, pensive. But I don't think you're doing it well, being supportive and all.

The therapist crossed one hand over the other hand and her eyes rested unreadably on Gil. She turned to Irene.

Irene, can you think why Gil should need my support?

All right, I see your game, said Gil. But just to be clear, I do not feel your support.

I don't either, said Irene.

You don't? Gil made a little move toward Irene.

But I don't care, said Irene, severe. She was holding a large cup of coffee in her hands. I do not need her support. You're the one who needs her support.

All right, said Gil. I do need her support, then! I *am* fighting for my family, can you see? For the unity of our family.

The therapist looked at him penetratingly, then turned her gaze upon Irene.

Gil spoke very softly to retrieve the therapist's attention. I'd like to start over. Could starting over be the problem?

Is Irene having trouble starting over? Is Irene afraid to start over?

I'm not going to start over again, said Irene. I've started over a thousand times. These times were never obvious to you until I decided to quit starting over anymore. I will never start over with you. I just want it to be over now. I want you to let me go. Share the children. Don't make everybody suffer.

You know I can't do that, said Gil. Because I love you.

Why do you love me, anyway?

Fuck you, said Gil. He sounded sincere, not angry. I wish I didn't. I'm just made this way.

He stared down at his lap and looked depressed.

Irene, he said after a moment, I thought you wanted to come in here about the paintings, my paintings of you.

Forget the paintings. Why can't we just separate, divorce, amicably, or amiably, like other people?

That is a myth, Irene.

It is not a myth, is it? Irene appealed to the therapist, who opened her mouth to answer, but Gil spoke first.

I don't think I'm the father of the children. I think that Irene let the truth slip out at our last session, or at our first session.

It was our only session, said Irene. She stared hard at Gil.

The therapist did not move or change her expression. She seemed nerveless, regarding them with equal interest.

Gil found her lack of affect so eerie that he almost shouted at her and at Irene, both.

Why don't you say something?

Okay, Irene said. I will say something. Gil, I told you I was kidding about that remark, and that it was mean, very mean. I apologized. I went over the line. The children are yours, of course!

Irene's stare became hurt concern. She wondered if she could corner him, here in front of the therapist, who seemed much more formidable today. She wanted to trap Gil into admitting that he had been reading her diaries.

Gil's mouth dropped open and he shook his head, as if to clear his vision.

Irene! They're not my children, all right? I know.

Why do you think this? said the therapist. Don't you believe Irene?

I do not.

Then it is a question of trust, said the therapist. Irene, are you telling the truth?

Of course I am! I'll admit it was hard to forgive, what I said, but it was just words, Gil.

Just words? Irene, you blurted out the truth and now you're backing away. Tell me the truth.

They're your children.

They are not.

Please calm down, said the therapist. Leaving aside the issue of the children, for now, let's try to get at the basis of your lack of mutual trust.

Yes, said Irene, why don't you trust me, Gil?

Perhaps we should consider paternity testing, he said with an acid smile.

That's sick, said Irene. I think that's low. Taking blood. They hate needles.

It's a DNA test. Just a cheek swab. No biggie, Irene.

Irene rolled her eyes. All right, Gil. I have no objection for paternity testing to be added into their regularly scheduled checkups. They will at least be prepared.

Gil dropped his face into his hands.

Oh, shit. Yes, fine. Can you imagine? We know two of the doctors in the practice socially.

You know them, said Irene. I don't know anybody.

Poor you. Can you imagine the buzz?

Irene laughed. Right, especially when it turns out they each have a different father.

Go on. Gil's face went red and his teeth clamped together. Go on, Irene.

What?

Three different fathers.

Hey, that was the joke! A very bad pathetic joke for which I again apologize. They are yours, Gil.

No.

I'm getting tired of this, said Irene to the therapist. Can we move on?

Gil, said the therapist, can we move on?

No.

Gil grabbed a handful of Kleenex and put them to his face.

He sobbed, a deep, dry, heaving sob. He spoke from out of the fluttering tissues.

She is untrustworthy and I do not believe her.

I have never deceived you, said Irene.

He took the tissues away. His face was red and swollen. His neat ponytail was coming undone. Strands of gray hair hung down around his ears.

You're deceiving me right now. I don't think it, I know it.

Why? said the therapist.

Why? said Irene to Gil. Why? How can you say this of me? You're crazy! Where is your proof, Gil? She jabbed her finger at him. She was imperious, sharp, witchlike in her heavy makeup. Quit making accusations and just let me go. Let's just separate. Things will get better that way.

No. Absolutely not.

Why?

He didn't answer.

Is it the paintings, Gil? It won't matter. This will be absorbed into the paintings. You said it. Art absorbs everything. I will continue to sit for you, if you want.

Gil gave her a look of despairing scorn. Do you think you're essential to my work? Do you? I'd be better off without you, Irene. Gil stared down at his hands and shook his head in helpless misery.

Listen, Gil. She spoke softly. If you think that the children aren't yours, you can't love me. You shouldn't. You shouldn't even want to be around me. Us. Why don't you let me go, since I'm so untrustworthy? Why don't you let me take the children with me, since they aren't yours?

Irene's face was naked, filling suddenly with hope. She touched his arm. Gil looked up and his self-pity dropped away. He was riveted. He frowned in concentration. He strained toward her. For a long time, he did not speak. The room was silent. His eyes flickered. He blinked at her.

I see, he said at last. Yes, I see now! I get it. He nodded, sat back, looked down with a mocking grimace of admiration.

Yes, yes. Nicely done.

The back of Irene's neck prickled.

Gil smoothed his hair back, brushed at his shirt. His tears vanished. His face abruptly turned neutral, cold.

Are you going to tell us what you're thinking? said Irene.

I don't think I will. Gil gave her a twisted little smile of affection. You really *are* clever, Irene. Much more clever than people think. You really had me.

Please explain, said the therapist. Because you've lost me.

I don't think we need to explain ourselves to you, said Gil. You're just a functionary of some kind here. You're just the dumb catalyst. She's the one. He wagged his finger at Irene, smiling openly now. She's the one. His eyes glittered with praise. She took me for a ride. She took me for a long ride. His voice expanded.

Quiet down, said Irene.

Gil wagged his finger at her again. So when did you know? When did you first suspect? How long have you had me going?

Irene's stomach hollowed, but she couldn't help responding to his admiration.

Oh, oh, Irene, there is a smile stuffed down there. Come on, you're proud of yourself. You know you are. Come on . . . he touched her arm.

Irene, said the therapist. What is happening to you right now? It was as if her voice came down to Irene from the top of a well.

Irene, stay with yourself, said the therapist.

Stay with yourself, Gil mocked. Irene's eyes were stuck to Gil's face. She had already started laughing and soon she was laughing so hard that her throat shut and she had to gasp for breath. She stood up, reeling. She had to let Gil help her.

Stand your ground, said the therapist, who rose with them but did not move.

Bill me double, said Gil, this was worth every minute. He steered Irene out, still laughing, through the discreet little side door. Irene could only waggle her fingers as the door shut.

They tried to cram back their laughter all the way to the car, but it kept escaping in snorts and grunts. When they got into the car, they exploded. They screamed with laughter. They could not stuff it back. Slowly, Gil drove home. They walked hand in hand into the empty house. It would be hours before the children returned from school. Irene pressed against Gil. He gripped her arm and she came up the stairs with him. He took off her coat when they entered his studio. They were not laughing now. He shut the door behind her, roughly cupped her face in his palms, and kissed her. He put his tongue in her mouth and their kiss deepened. But he stopped, drew away, and looked at her searchingly.

So when did you know? When did you first suspect? His voice was intimate.

The dogs started barking downstairs. Irene started, looked at the door.

It's nothing, said Gil.

She reached past Gil. He grabbed her arm and took her hand off the doorknob.

Irene. We're going to talk about this. We're going to have this out. This is going to be our little truth session. We're going to tell each other everything.

She reached past him again. He took her hand off the knob again. She put her hand out a third time, and he struck her arm away.

Irene!

She didn't move. She rubbed her arm. I don't know what you're talking about, she said.

Yes you do. You knew all along that I was reading your diaries. You knew, didn't you? That's why you wrote those things. To hurt me, to get even, to manipulate me. You had me! But I'm sorry. I'll never do it again.

Do what?

Read your diaries.

Irene suddenly gave him the same look she had given him the morning Stoney was born, when he had wanted to check the television. A mask came off, he'd thought, that time. But this time it was worse. She straightened and seemed to grow until she was taller than him. A black energy scored the air. She bared her teeth. The whites of her eyes showed all around the iris. Hatred beamed out of her.

You've been reading my diaries? For how long? How many years? Since the beginning?

You didn't know? You didn't write those things to hurt me?

Of course not, she whispered. She touched him lightly on the arm, and he stepped away from the door.

They had promised to take the children to the frozen river that night for winter fireworks. There were people crowded all along the banks. They arrived late and Gil, with a burst of manic despair, insisted on pushing to the front of the crowd and stepping over the restraining fence, then down the bank into unstable snow, where he spread a quilt, bending back the leafless wiry tangle of grape and lythrum. They lowered themselves gingerly onto the blanket, digging their snow-booted heels through the cloth or pushing their feet against the massed undergrowth to keep from sliding down. The spit of land that had been Spirit Island, where the fireworks display was set up and ready to be touched off, was directly across from them; and immediately the fireworks began, raining down showers of gel-like fire so close that the children flinched thrillingly and ever afterward remembered that night not only as the night Florian found the cat, but as the best fireworks they'd ever seen. There were two displays, really, the one that filled the sky and its exact reflection in the flat black ice of the Mississippi. The grand finale was a fusillade of sparks and explosions that enchanted and slightly deafened them so that, as they sat for a while longer, swigging hot chocolate from Irene's metal-tasting thermos and eating handfuls of trail mix from a bag she'd brought in her purse, they almost didn't hear it. Then Stoney shrieked. An animal had brushed his legs. Irene pulled him up, thinking of rats, but at the same time Riel saw the shape and Florian put his hand out. The frail cat vanished, but stayed in the dark snow, complaining.

Come on, Irene said, brisk. Let's go now. Leave it.

No! Florian was already down on all fours.

It's hungry, said Riel. It'll freeze.

Here! Stoney bent and held out his peanuts.

We're out of here, said Gil, pulling Riel along.

But Riel, who would normally have folded obediently or stiffened under her father's touch, turned on him in a cool fury and shoved him with all her strength. Gil stumbled in surprise and lurched into a tangle of vines that held his feet. He fell heavily, but was too shocked, and then too embarrassed, even too distracted by hopelessness, to lash out. He rose slowly, and said nothing. Riel had Florian's knitted scarf off, already, to catch the cat. Florian reached behind the cat's head, picked it up by the nape of the neck, and lifted it toward his chest. At first it hissed and spat, but it was clearly relieved to be held and once Florian bundled it tight under the scarf the cat quieted and crept closer. The children knew that Irene did not like cats, but she would be helpless in the face of anything that they wanted as fervently as they now wanted this cat.

Although no one else in the family had seen Riel push her father, they all sensed immediately that Gil's opinion was now of no concern.

Put it down, said Irene. But Florian didn't. Instead, he smiled into his mother's face and said, Oh, Mom, just touch him. He's purring.

Irene didn't care if she was being swayed. She wanted Florian to love her again.

The moment she put her hand out, the children knew that they would be able to keep the cat and they clustered close to Florian and took turns feeling the soft whir in the cat's starved, striped body.

On the way back from the fireworks, Gil stopped at an all-night Walgreens and Irene bought cat supplies. At home, Florian put the cat box in the basement and let the cat scratch around in it. He took the cat to bed with him. Gravely and stiffly, the cat edged along the pillows, sniffing one and then the next, fixing

Florian with its yellow alien stare. At last it settled incremen-
tally on the pillow next to his head, and a soft, broken rattle
started in its throat. Florian turned on his side and watched the
cat, without touching it, then gradually closed his eyes.

Riel lay in her room that night, on top of the bedclothes,
awake in the dark, staring up at the ceiling. Again she felt the
surge of heavy surprise that had flashed through her when her
father's body had yielded, when he had stumbled, and when
he'd not struck back. She'd gone straight to her room and
hadn't taken off her clothes yet for fear he'd realize what had
happened and she'd be yanked from the bed. If he came to get
her, she would be ready. But when the house fell silent and still
nothing happened, she began to breathe, slowly breathe. She
pulled her warm comforter up to her neck. Her eyes and throat
began to prickle, and suddenly her face was wet with emotion.
If she had succeeded, if she had taken away his power, then she
was very much alone and responsible for everyone.

Irene took the cat to the vet the next day and learned it had
worms, three other types of parasites, plus fleas, ticks, pink-

eye, and a possible lung infection. The vet's bill came to almost a thousand dollars. Gil asked, Why did you pay it?

What would you have done? said Irene.

They turned around. Florian had entered the room with his yellow cat.

His name is Schrodinger, he said.

Oh, said Gil, like the Peanuts character?

No, said Florian. This would be Schrodinger with an umlaut. The physicist. Haven't you ever heard of Schrödinger's dilemma?

How pretentious, said Gil. The mere sight of the cat infuriated him. What a pretentious little shit you are!

Florian stroked the cat, put his face down into its fur, then looked at his mother and raised his eyebrows.

Irene took a deep breath. Florian went away with the cat.

That's it, said Irene. Get out of this house.

Get out of my house? Gil began to laugh. Irene, you're too much. I thought we were supposed to support each other, be unified, a couple around the children at least. I thought that was supposed to be the healthy thing to do.

Irene's eyes filled, she twisted her hands in her shirt. Just go, she said again.

No, you go! Gil spread his arms. You go! You! He whirled in a circle. My work paid for this. My blood! He smacked his hands together and showed her his palms.

Irene started and didn't move.

Whatever you did to your hands, she said at last, you still have to go.

Wow, he said in a softly dangerous voice, I guess you think you mean it. He stood as if arrested with the thought. As he stood there, a wildly ambitious longing took hold of him. He put out his arms and fell to his knees and said in a gasp:

I just want you to love me. I feel like I'm suffocating in my skin. I am so alone without you, Irene. Touch me, please touch me.

Irene stepped away.

Oh god, said Gil.

She went to him and lay her hand on his hair and began to stroke it. He put his arms around her leg, held her leg very gently, then lowered his forehead to the side of her knee.

Irene's fingers balled into a fist. She struck him such a hard blow to the temple that he nearly tipped over.

She stood frozen. Her fist hung at her side, a stinging weight.

Gil righted himself, took hold of her leg again, cupped her fist in his hand. He kissed her curled fingers.

Irene cried out and shook her hand free. Riel had come into the room.

Is Daddy okay? she asked. She looked down at her father in dread. She had seen it all.

Gil, said Irene, get up. She shook his arm off her leg and stepped toward Riel.

I'm sorry, said Riel to her mother, and she fell forward and buried her face in Irene's blouse. Her head came to right beneath Irene's breasts. When Irene put her arms around her, she didn't have to bend over anymore. Gil got to his feet and Irene felt Riel's arms tighten, but he just walked silently out of the entryway, then into the kitchen. They heard the cupboard open, then the refrigerator door's cold yawn, the clatter of ice from the ice maker, the trickle of liquid. They heard Gil's steps ascending to his studio.

Mom, said Riel, her face still hidden and her voice muffled, don't divorce him.

They stood together in the tall light of the curved old windows. Riel was breathing right against Irene's heart. Her wiry arms were clasped hard around Irene's waist, meeting at the back. There was a powerful odor of outside air, snow, and sunlight on Riel's hair.

I might have to, Irene said. Really, I might.

No, said Riel.

I think . . . said Irene.

No, said Riel.

But maybe . . . said Irene.

Please, said Riel.

Gil drove off to sit with his Lucretia, but it was afternoon and there was a class of college students in the room. And so instead he visited *The Dining Room in the Country*, painted in 1913 by Pierre Bonnard. A glowing blue door opens inward. The walls are an intense burnt orange. The landscape is fuming brilliance and his wife peers in over the sill. It is spring. The leaves are just forming in the branches.

A formal velvet swag of rope just before the painting kept mesmerized viewers from stumbling into it. Gil stood behind the rope.

All his life, Bonnard had painted little moments, *intimisme*, a child playing with sand, pets alert to food on the table. And there was Marthe. Her sinuous little body, his ideal. He had painted her indolent after sex, shimmering and dreaming in the bath, peering in the window beside that inward-opening blue door. By most accounts she was a peevish shrew, and yet Bonnard had loved her with his art. His world had narrowed with the war. He'd lost his wife. During that time, he had painted a self-portrait that Gil found both unbearable and heroic. In this picture of himself alone, frail, old, staring into the bathroom mirror, Bonnard had used every color. His eyes were deep, all-seeing, steady. Every color he had used in his life was there in that self-portrait. It was a portrait of the artist's gathered spirit, the self wearily dissolving into weariless color and light. He was bald as an egg and yet his naked skull was still caressed here and there by a bit of radiance, a rind of sun.

Together in Paris, he and Irene had stared at this portrait and, for different reasons, wept.

Part III

❄

December 15, 2007

Irene sat in the car, outside the house. The divorce papers were clipped together in a plain envelope on the seat beside her. She had left the children with Louise. One of the dogs braced his feet on the couch by the window and stared out at her, his ears alert.

You know, she said, don't you. She held the dog's gaze.

She called out as she walked into the house and her voice sounded reassuringly ordinary.

I'm on the phone, answered Gil from upstairs.

She waited at the beautiful dining room table, the falsely distressed wood, full of fake wormholes, each flaw polished and deepened as though by generations of family dinners. There was a fork left on the table. She punched lightly at the wood. The mirror that had once scared Florian seemed to waver on the wall, full of drowsy shadows.

I'm still waiting, she called up the stairs after a while. He had forgotten about her. There was a scrambled burst of conversation, then good-byes.

So what is it?

He was wary and reserved. They had barely spoken for the last day.

Sit down. Please. Will you please sit down?

He saw the plain envelope.

What's that?

Irene told him.

A smile bloomed, his head cocked to the side, his hands gripped the chair. He sagged. Knocked off his feet. He went down on his knees. He kept on kneeling there for a while, then got up like nothing had happened and sent the dogs from the room and closed the door.

No, she said, leave the dogs in.

Okay, those are divorce papers. This is a surprise.

He said it over again, wiping his face. He threw his hands out, toward Irene. She stepped away. The dogs started barking behind the door. Redness crept up his neck, up the sides of his ears. Up behind his glasses.

I'm so sorry, she said, though she'd promised herself not to say it.

Are you? Are you?

He stretched his arms out. Waved his hands at the papers.

Take them back!

He was wearing a dark red knit shirt and Irene was astounded upon touching him, trying to get by him to open the door, to find his shirt was completely wet. How did he do this? His whole body cried when he cried. He carefully put his arms around her and then tightened his arms until he held her so hard that she could barely breathe.

I don't care about him. He hissed into her hair. I don't care about any of them. As for the papers, I do not accept them. I will not sign them. You will not go.

She tried to struggle away, but he toppled her slowly in an awkward tackle. He was weeping in a gut-wrenched way, with whining groans like tree roots pulled from the ground.

I don't care about them, I don't care, he chanted, tightening his grip. She tried to twist out from under him, pushed, rocked against him, smashed at him. It was like grappling with a great, padded couch. He had made himself enormous, impervious.

He put his weight on the arm he held across her chest, pinned her legs with his legs. With his other hand he pulled her jeans down her hips. The dogs scratched at the door. She tried to tear at him but he felt nothing. He pried her legs apart with his knees, and then, still weeping steadily, he began to caress her. She tried to hold herself stiffly away from him. But he stopped crying and his anger flowed up her throat. He crushed her jeans down past her knees, stared at her for a moment in hatred and then forced himself into her, pushing her along the floor. He didn't come until he'd banged her head against the wall and she didn't come until later, when she had dragged herself upstairs. She walked into the bathroom, locked the door, and took off her clothes. She stood dazed; after a few minutes she ran her bath and slid in. Alone in hot steam, in the bathtub, she came so many times she got a cramp in her hand and started laughing.

What's going on in there, said Gil, tenderly, at the door.

Maybe nothing had happened, she thought, floating her hips up to her hand again. How will I explain my carpal tunnel syndrome to the hand surgeon? I'll blame it on writing an entire dissertation in longhand. I'll say I wrote a hundred drafts.

If only he would die, she thought, as he rapped lightly on the door.

I'm bringing up champagne, he said. If you unlock the door, I'll push it in on a tray. I promise I won't come in.

I don't want any, she said.

Oh yes, you do. Cold champagne in a hot bath? You do.

Yes, Irene thought. I do. But maybe he is going to kill me, drown me. Or maybe he will turn on the hair dryer and throw it in the tub. Maybe he will slice my wrists and stage my suicide. These are just things a paranoid woman would think.

Listen, he said. I'll tie a string to the tray. You can pull it toward you. I won't come in.

She stepped out of the tub, unlocked the door, then got back into the water. The door opened slightly and he threw a piece of twine at the bathtub, pushed the tray in—the champagne flute was lying side down on a napkin. On the tray there was an ice bucket holding an opened bottle with a cloth napkin wrapped around the lip. Next to it there was a small silver bowl of caviar on crushed ice, another of sour cream, and a stack of water crackers. The door closed. Irene stared at the arrangement. Actually, she thought, he is staging my suicide. There. The cord was attached to the handle of the tray and she reached down, grabbed the end, and pulled it toward the tub. When the champagne was close enough, she grasped the bottle by the neck. A thread of mist curled from its lip. The bottle was graceful and expensive. Made of heavy green glass. The crisp brown lettering on the label was ornate and festive. She held the sweating bottle by the throat. She had always thought that when she really quit it would be a supreme act of will taking endless forethought. But it wasn't. Her hand tipped the bottle. Irene watched the champagne, pale and cold, dry and golden, flow down her breasts.

Denial shatters like glass. At the bottom of the stairs to his studio, Gil thought: We'll all take a trip together. We'll go to Mexico. We'll find tickets online. A charter. It will be a surprise for everybody. I'll present this to them. She cannot deny the children. He reached the top of the staircase. The cat, Schrodinger with an umlaut, sat gravely on the top step. The cat was rangy, sallow, and in its eyes there glowed a golden silence. Gil had never had a cat and found them deceptive, uncanny. That the cat should sit coolly on the threshold to his studio made his skin crawl. The cat did not belong there, and yet it morbidly challenged him. They stared at each other as Gil mounted the steps. At one point, their eyes were level and Gil experienced a dreamlike jolt of terror. He cried out. The cat flew into the air at the sound. It seemed to vanish, whisked away like a stage ghost. Gil had no idea where it went, and found that he was shivering when he entered his studio. He locked the door behind him and then curled up on his daybed, staring out the window. He drew over himself the lush green blanket upon which he'd painted Irene, but he couldn't get warm. His teeth clacked together. I suppose it's shock, he thought. She has not loved me for a long time. There is nothing I can do. I am incapable of taking care of the children. They will leave me and take the dogs. The awful cat.

A crushing darkness welled up from under the mopboards; it crept heavily from the walls, descended in drags from the ceiling. He hadn't known the air could weigh so much. He closed his eyes and was forced into a black sulcus that kept tightening until he could not move.

Irene heard Gil pacing upstairs the first night, and she locked the bedroom door. She knew that Gil had food up in his studio, water, lots of booze, a toilet. He could in fact live up there if he wanted to. The next morning, she called Louise and told her everything.

Are you from the planet stupid, Irene? He raped you. Call the police and get out of there.

It wasn't exactly, I . . . can you keep the kids another night?

No.

Then I'll come and get them.

Okay, of course I'll keep them, Irene.

You're pissed off at me.

Irene, call the police.

I can't do that to him.

Oh my god! I feel like beating the shit out of you myself!

Louise hung up.

Irene saw white shadows falling past the window, one after the next. She went outside. Gil had tossed out six paintings, two on canvas, four on heavy wooden panels. Her portraits had landed in thick snow and were not damaged. She carried them one by one into the garage. As she was lifting the last painting out, there was a ringing noise beside her. Gil had thrown down an empty vodka bottle. She looked up and dodged a blur. Another hit just to her left. She hurried out of range and took the long way around so that she didn't pass beneath Gil's studio windows. The next morning, there were four empty bottles in the snow, their naked throats cheerily askew. Later, there were five, then six, and by evening she had stopped hearing Gil move. She knocked on the door to his studio. He had never given her a key. She put her hand on the door and called his name.

Part IV

❄

December 26, 2007

RED DIARY

T he children took things too well, acted with a
buoyant unconcern. It took the death of Snowball the guinea pig on Christmas Eve to bring them
down. Then again. Not only was this little white creature the class guinea pig, therefore iconic, like some
sort of little tribal totem, but she was much beloved
by Stoney himself who was chosen as though by the
gods, plucked from the common mass of first graders,
to bring Snowball home during the long winter break
when anything can happen.

Xmas Eve. You in treatment. Me relieved you are
safe, and gone. For a time I did not care if I had driven
you crazy. I had no time to care. I did not understand
how everything was tied to you, organized, tethered.
Cut loose, we drift. Seized by giddiness, we drag food

out and eat whatever we want, whenever we want. We stay up late. We camp out in sleeping bags alongside the dogs. At some point I know I've got to take control and make the rules and set boundaries and return to a routine, but not yet. The season of peace and chaos is upon us and our children are beginning to talk to me. They always did talk to me, but this is different. I suppose me not drunk is different. They tell me everything. They forget I am there. They talk and talk about their insanely complex subculture—Florian's obsessed with dark matter and Riel recounts a teenage witch movie I do not remember letting her watch where girls bite veins of sadistic gym teachers and eat fresh guinea pigs—what now?

Say you were me?

A mother's brain is an ort pile where the cultural guano of the ages of each of her children survives. A composted yellow slick on the bottom of Big Bird feathers and Barbie hair cut with Crayola scissors and old plastic marker tubes and Tweety card decks, tiny little shoes, purses, belts, shimmery underwear and skates for Barbie and then the more politically correct stuff made of wood, the popsicle stick dolls and the blocks in every shape, painted, the wooden horses and the sets of foot-piercing dangerous jacks and red rubber balls and the miniature horses and the coveted big plastic horses and the Playmobil and Legos and action figures and math toys and sets of mazes and puzzles from about twelve dozen sets and the stuffed things— tigersnakelephantarantulapepigiraffeturtleagle—and the marvelous tea sets that come in every china pattern and the little furniture and mirrors, the detritus of vintage Star Ponies and Wild Things and Seuss figurines and every McDonald's Happy Meal toy and then, well, all of this compacted together with old Halloween candy mortise into a solid-earthen basement floor of kid knowledge.

My mind is a toy basket filled with tiny, cheap, broken stuff.

But that afternoon, anyway, that blessed xMas eve late afternoon anticipating night when I'm trying to stop the euphoria from overflowing—Louise and her good-hearted partner come bearing gifts and towing their rescued greyhound. We let the pale red greyhound pace elegantly through the house and are drinking a cup of chai when suddenly we hear these hellish shrieks—ringing through the house—guinea pig trauma noises, and a noise like that from a silent inoffensive thing is truly terrible to hear.

Instantly we all know something very bad has occurred. And now the dog is tiptoeing from Stoney's room with the guinea pig in his beautiful long greyhound mouth. This dog's powerful lithe haunches are quivering as he looks to us for approval since, yes, he was trained to do this *n'est ce pas?* I mean, his look says, Wasn't I chasing one of these things all my life? And we shout at him and retrieve the shrieking furball and quickly wrap it in the arms of Stoney, who in turn transfers the creature, with a look of penetrating trust, to me.

This morning, as I do every morning, I was feeling utterly forsaken in the universe. I was enjoying the feeling of this whopping self-pity and I was afraid. My gladness had slowly been penetrated by the understanding that I was the one adult in charge of three complicated, innocent children, who, in turn, had begun to slowly realize that their father was not coming back for a long time, either to frighten or to save them. What would that mean? They looked at me, stuck.

I missed my mother with a steady ache. But since I couldn't turn things over to her, I began to imagine that another Irene, someone stronger and saner, would walk into the room and tell me to go back to sleep. She'd take care of things from now on. I knew there was no way I could do everything without a drink. Bring the children to school. Check in with your treatment coach. Call the lawyers. Pick the crap up. The house had suddenly gone feral. Junk was everywhere. Trash. Recycling. Bins of old bottles with their thirsty uncapped mouths. Inside, of course I knew that I was the one who had to do it all. However, every morning last week after you left I asked for help from my mother, who could not answer, and then pretended I was Nurse Irene.

Nurse Irene came in and took over with efficiency and calm and left the real Irene whimpering beneath the covers.

Calm down, said Nurse Irene, in faintly irritated patience. Drink this laudanum and I'll get them off to school.

Then, as I did every morning, I got up and tried to rouse the children in iron dark Minnesota solid cold—for school—insane laughter—searching out clean socks and loose enough necked turtlenecks and mittens, books, homework. All of these things that the normal ever-sober mother, whose children are not maniacally happy and furiously sad by turns, has trouble finding anyway. I hung on, scratched out the hours until vacation.

Oh Nurse Irene, my toast has got all cold and tough. Please, take it away!

So I have the guinea pig curled on my stomach the way you warm a hypothermia victim—because though outwardly unhurt she is twitching. Her rodent teeth are clenched. Her gentle, foolish eyes squeezed shut and turning blue around the edges. She is going into shock. Nose cold. Bad signs. Bad omens. We have crawled under a feather comforter and I am sending all of my energy into the guinea pig because the scariest thing is that Stoney believes simply and fervently that once this creature is in my arms it will be absolutely fine. *Snowball, oh, Snowball*, I mentally plead, *do not die.* You mean a great deal to a lot of people on this night of the holy beasts. Your little life on earth is plenty difficult I know, but must it come to this? Yes, I have heard that some of the other first graders drop you or they squeeze you. I have been told you are apt to poop in their laps. And now this greyhound rescued from lethal injection at the dog tracks has finally, after chasing little animals his whole life through, caught one and it was you. And instead of good dog pats he is met with the shock and horror of the alphas. It was wrong, little one, it should not have happened. But to let go of all that is precious and perfect on the night of nights? Must it be? If not for yourself, little fur thing, then please for my tender son stay alive and frisk about. Frisk about! But I can feel the thing itself lose the spark of life and I know exactly when Snowball dies.

And in that moment I decide I am nevertheless very fortunate because I have a credit card and that card hasn't quite hit the limit and I have a phone book with yellow pages and a pet store section and it is 4 P.M. xmAs Eve and not 5 P.M. and although I have one dead guinea pig in my armpit and it is -20 degrees outside, you encouraged me last fall to put a new battery in my car and it will start.

Calmly, very calmly, I speak to the children.

Dear children, I say, we must go on a quest to find a fellow guinea pig to cuddle with Snowball and bring her back to us for she is *in shock*. I signal Florian and Riel with my eyes. They signal back. We don't say dead, not yet, not until we have another little life in this house. It is amazing with what dispatch the three, one of whom must be hand-dressed for school, the oldest of whom scorns any form of punctuality, can ready themselves, bundling madly, when there is a new guinea pig to fetch. In coats and boots and brilliant striped gloves we are out the door. Louise and Bobbi and the greyhound slouch morosely off toward the relief of a stable holiday. I leave Snowball in her doll blanket on top of the warm tumbling dryer because you never know—who is the resurrection and the light? Who understands the physiology of class pets?

It all seems too much without a bottle of something, anything, even that old flask of Jägermeister I let trickle down the sink two days ago, and yet I am told by earnest bearers of 12-step literature that we can take what is shoveled onto our backs. There is some sort of plan here—the following: God gives us nothing we are not strong enough to bear.

Not me. Good thing I have Nurse Irene.

So while wondering as I will do every day of my life exactly what I will do without a drink, I decide we will definitely find a new guinea pig and this xmaS will go on as even the beasts must talk.

We have liftoff. They are just shutting down the guinea pig store but we barge in with desperate cries and money and he is there, oh, he is there. Color of a ripe apricot. Cinnamon. Little cream fur swatches on him. Peachy boy. Spice boy. Totoro Baby. Ours. And we go home with him in a cardboard box, on the quietly worshipping lap of Stoney, and once at home, once there, the death of Snowball although sad does not devastate. For life is burgeoning. Up all around us. In the stillness. In the heat. In the christbirthing pinecone air.

———

Snowball. Snowball. Pig of pigs. I am culpable. Gil. You said everything was kitsch. That French music critic with his stacks of CDs was kitsch. Therefore, I see it now, believable. I half-believe in the French

music critic myself looking into Stoney's green eyes—
his eyes lighted up with joy for the little creature in
his lap. Will I insist to you now that you are your
children's father? Sure. But the deception as I see it
was only inevitable. Something had to happen. One
of us go crazy. And as you see from this entry, I may
be cracking too. Yet I thank the christchild that upon
returning to this house with one live guinea pig and
(I check) one stiff dead one on the dryer wrapped up
in a doll blanket, split guinea pig lip lifted over bony
teeth, we are yet in the presence of the strange form
of grace even cynics call love and I remember how
hard you worked and how dutiful you were and how
you wrapped all of your christmas gifts with unusual
papers and used a ruler to measure out these papers
and affixed to the perfectly wrapped and extravagant
gifts flowing ribbons of real silk or satin-leaved flowers and how you loved us, marred by anger, how you
hated yourself, marred by vanity, and how you loved
us. Like crazy. In a mean way. But love is love. How
all of that got mixed so that on the holiest of unholy
nights I can call your confiscated number and whisper into the phone, Please don't kill yourself. Live on.
Endure.

When they broke into your studio they found you'd
nearly poisoned yourself with the vodka left over from
the party—all of the bottles down in the snow that

missed me. But you didn't die. So live on, Gil. Endure. Because you cannot ever be replaced and to kill yourself means never having to say you're sorry. No, no. Love means that you must adamantly cling to life. Love means being there to take it. Your children, even the sarcastic oldest boy, are playing with their new guinea pig and waiting for the dead one to come back to life on this night of reprieves. I've got the dead one going in the dryer, all fluffed out and warm, thinking maybe that's CPR for a guinea pig who died of no wound but fear, yes, the teeth around him stopped his mild little heart as lies do. Live on. Live on. I am calling you I am the nurse and I bring you this cup of warm broth and I am telling you drink it.

Part V

❄

L ate May. Gil had moved back into the house the week before, and on Memorial Day weekend the family piled into the larger of the two cars and traveled four hours to Bayfield, Wisconsin. The ice had gone out late in the spring and Lake Superior was too cold for swimming. There, waiting for the ferry to Madeline Island, Irene smiled for the first time and Florian took the iPod buds from his ears and calmly surveyed the shattered sun on the surface of the icy lake.

I have no conviction whatsoever that this is going to be all right, said Florian, looking at the water.

It's all dark matter, Puon, said Riel, thinking of her book.

Stoney let his father pick him up, Riel slouched up next to her mother, Florian returned the buds to his ears and scrolled down to In Utero. Together they watched the great white boat from the island approach the dock.

The place they borrowed had been constructed over many summers by a man who'd grown old putting the finishing touches on a house with a great fieldstone fireplace. He had used barn board, driftwood, irregular salvage. The door handles were made of antlers, spools, curved and polished branches. Off the great, rough, weathered dock the shore was rocky but there was a small beach to one side and a half-moon of tawny sand. This early in the season, when the driftwood had collected all fall and winter, there were un-touched snags of refuse to comb through. The children built huts of curved boards, silver roots, and Irene made a fire pit. They sat there at dusk, watching the transparent flames. She and Gil did most things without talking. Silence between them was a way of trying. Gil had grown very thin and let his hair trail long. He did not look like the man he was last year, nor like the man she had married. He did not look like anyone she had ever seen before.

She had told him that there wasn't going to be any sex. That's over, she said. It will be years before I let you sleep with me. Or paint me. He looked puzzled, and thought she was absurdly out of touch for thinking those things could interest him now. When he'd stopped drinking, he'd stopped eating, and when he'd stopped eating, he'd stopped wanting anything. In the late afternoon, when his energy flagged, he slept or sat still and gave attention to transitory noises and sensations. He'd started living in his body, which he'd always hated for disgracing him—by wanting Irene too much, but somehow not in the right way, or wanting to paint her more than make love to her sometimes. He'd despised his body for its boring hungers, reflex anger; its petty, obliterating rage. But now he'd become detached. He regarded his body with a tender regret. It was a thing his spirit had to haul.

On the third morning, he lay on a towel and let warm sand trickle through his fingers over and over. Only the lightest insects had hatched, fairylike flies that the breeze blew off. The sun was a rich bloodred through the skin of his eyelids. His children's voices, absorbed in their construction work, rose and fell with the waves. Far offshore, there were the broken cries of gulls. To exist in his body, in such ease, at that time. This was the best moment of his life.

He got up and walked over to his children. Florian shook his hug off and Riel froze when he touched her hair. He kissed Stoney's sun-warm forehead and let him go back to his play. Then Gil waded up to his thighs in the fierce, clean water. His feet were already half numb when he dived, absorbed the shock, and began to swim. Behind him, the dogs were barking in concern. He'd go as far as he could. A few minutes of swimming should be enough to drop his body temperature to a level from which he could not recover. At first, he seemed to bob on the transparent waves; then suddenly his arms turned to lead bats. Soon they would be impossible to lift. The children would run to Irene. She would understand what he was doing, and keep them from witnessing the outcome. She would call Island Rescue to retrieve his body. Irene. He thought of her lugubrious rendition of The Wreck of the Edmund Fitzgerald. *The legend lives on from the Chippewa on down . . . the lake it is said never gives up her dead . . .* he started laughing and choked and knew his brain was slowing. Treading water, he turned for a last look and saw her.

Irene was standing on the silver dock with her hand raised, waiting. She called his name, and called again, and so he turned obediently and started for her, beating the water back, but he seemed to stay in one place no matter how hard he kicked. He saw his arms lift and pull but he couldn't feel them, still he kept going and when he peered ahead she was there, waiting for him, so he surged forward, and she was still there, again, when he looked, and he fought to move ahead, closer, again, moving toward her, until at last he saw her enter the waves.

Riel

After our mother waded into the lake and then threw herself forward and began to swim, we watched a moment, we hesitated. Then one of us cried out and we all—Florian, Stoney, and me, Riel—we all rushed into the knifelike cold. It sliced out our breath. Stoney could not go far and I struggled from the water with him, so numbed I couldn't think, and bitterly shaking. Florian got farther, but finally he quit, too. Out there, we saw, Mom was still swimming forward, her head out of water like a dog's. She didn't turn or make any sign that she noticed us at all. She just went to him. By the time she reached our father, he had floundered, but we saw her clutch his head and turn, dragging him by the hair. Her arm was straight out and she kicked, sidestroking. He was afloat behind her. We stood on the end of the silver dock. She was coming back to us—she had once showed us how you save someone: we knew what you do—and we had stopped crying. Then she disappeared. At first, we thought that she was swimming underwater. But then the dogs started barking in a different tone. A drawn-out sound almost like the braying of wild animals, and it struck us deeply. Stoney shrieked and I took the phone from the pocket of Mom's shirt where it was lying on her chair, and dialed 911.

When Florian hit the skids in high school, dropped out, and became addicted to everything he tried—booze, grass, cocaine, meth—Mom's sister, our aunt now, Louise, put him through treatment the first time. His high school teachers helped him through the second time. He is now in college. We talk. Last time, he told me that he was back into explaining the universe, and laughingly said he'd fried a few too many neurons and his classes were actually difficult. He's studying dark matter and supersymmetry again. He said that sometimes in human terms a broken supersymmetry—like his brain, our childhood, or the human face—can be the more elegant or at least more useful solution.

Solution to what? I said.

But he just smiled, one incisor crooked and black.

Stoney came out all right. He went to school in Hawaii, but he's on leave and I heard he went to Molokai and maybe wants to live there. I don't know exactly how. He doesn't often talk to me or Florian. He didn't like living with a big family, but I did. We grew up with Louise and Bobbi's family—we had a traditional adoption and I got brothers, sisters, twenty cousins, and it was all of them who mainly raised me. Which turned out to be a good thing, I think. I also found that the old-time Indians are us, still going to sundances, ceremonies, talking in the old language and even using the old skills if we feel like it, not making a big deal.

As for the dogs, they would still be alive if this was a movie. I haven't written down their names because if anything is sacred, they are. Do you understand? I'm not sure I do, but there it is. Snowball or one of his versions probably does live on in Stoney's old first-grade classroom yet. Schrodinger got fed a tab of acid and went down a storm drain. Pretty much, Florian always blamed himself.

Two years ago, just after I graduated from the University of Minnesota, and before I entered this graduate writing program, I turned twenty-one. On the day of my birthday, the lawyer who handled my parents' estate appeared at the doorway to the house. Gerald Oberfach is a good-natured, round sort of person with a hoarse, high-pitched voice, not the type at all you would think of as a tough lawyer. But he did a lot to shield us in those years following our parents' death. We just call him Ober.

Ober came into the house and asked if we could sit down and talk, alone. My sisters and brothers or cousins were in their rooms, and my aunts were gone somewhere. Things were quiet. I said sure and we walked into the cluttered, sunny kitchen. He sat down at the white table, which was flecked with gold glitter. I poured Ober a cup of coffee from the Mr. Coffee pot. He put a tiny red cardboard envelope on the table, and told me it was the key to a safe-deposit box. I just stared at it.

My feeling is that I don't want this, I said.

Ober drank the coffee and nodded, and nodded some more. He has the knack of saying nothing. But I could outlast him, and finally he had to speak.

Your mother told me that this should be given to you when you turned twenty-one. So . . .

I have been through a great deal of therapy, so it doesn't bother me anymore to say that I am angriest at my mother. The reason I am angriest at her is that she should have saved herself for us—not for him, for us. She died because she could not let go of him. But she should have let go, for us.

Yet I also know she thought she could save anyone, which makes it a stupid accident. So then I want to think she saw in our father's heart an unwavering light. Through all the shit-storms, a steady flame.

I can't decide.

I once asked Florian if an absolutely steady flame was possible. In an airless void, he said, an absolutely steady flame is theoretically possible and yet impossible. There would of course be no oxygen and without it a true fire could not exist.

I said to Ober again that I didn't want the key. Ober said I didn't have to take it, but he was leaving it all the same.

He gave me one of his overlong hugs, said good-bye, and walked out. The door closed and the key sat there. And I sat there, too, just looking at the key. Then not looking at the key. I was thinking of something else. For a long time, I just sat there, thinking.

All of a sudden, my sister or aunt or one of my cousins was making noise in the house, and I picked up the key. I put it in my pocket and I walked out the back door. It was early in the afternoon.

The address of the bank was printed on the little red envelope.

I hope there's lots of money in the box, I thought as I went there. But I knew there wouldn't be any money in the box. I think I knew that there would just be writing. And now, as you see, I have put it all together, both of her diaries. The Red Diary. The Blue Notebook. Her notes on Catlin. My memory charts. I have also filled in certain events and connections. Sometimes, it has helped me to talk to Louise. Other times, I imagined that I was my mother. Or my father. I have written about them in many ways. I interviewed their therapist, who decided it was better to serve the living than the dead, and went over her notes with me and laughed with me and cried. So you see, I am the third person in the writing. I am the one with the gift of omniscience, which is something—I don't know if it's generally known—that children develop once they lose their parents. This is also, of course, my master's thesis. I am a writer in a writing program and here is the place where I thank my mentors. Thank you, parents, you left me with your marriage, my material, the stuff of my life.

I am angriest at you, Mom, but there is this: you trusted me with the narrative.

I said that I was thinking after Ober left and as I stood in the warm dog-smelling kitchen. I was looking at the key, not knowing whether I would pick it up, leave it, or pick it up and throw it in the trash. Actually, I wasn't thinking, or deciding; I was remembering. I was caught in a memory I have had many times. It is always so real I lose track of what's around me and it seems to be happening again.

There are the crisp words on the phone, *Island Rescue Service*. Then the woman's voice telling me to go down the road and stand at the entrance to the cabin, so that the rescue crew will be sure to see me, or us, right away. And I remember my relief that there were instructions and something that would be done. And us looking back once at the shining surface of the great cold lake. We left the dock and climbed into the hooded dimness of the path, the tall birch and taller pines over us, and walked together until we came out of the dizzy green to the entrance, which was marked with an oar, printed with a fire number, lashed by an old rope to a pine. And I remember the three of us kids, the dogs with us, standing on the pavement of the broad warm highway that circled the island. And now as I remember it, I see it was midday, the sun right over us that day, and the pavement was hot on our feet, stinging hot, and it felt good, and it was noon and there were no shadows under us, or anywhere around us, it was all bright, flat, dazzling, and then the sirens began to rise and fall and grow louder in their rising and falling until they were here.

About the Author

Louise Erdrich is the author of thirteen novels as well as volumes of poetry, short stories, children's books, and a memoir of early motherhood. Her novel *Love Medicine* won the National Book Critics Circle Award. *The Last Report on the Miracles of Little No Horse* was a finalist for the National Book Award. Most recently, *The Plague of Doves* won the Anisfield-Wolf Book Award and was a finalist for the Pulitzer Prize. Louise Erdrich lives in Minnesota and is the owner of Birchbark Books, an independent bookstore.